Your Wild Heart

Black Hills Wolves Book 14

By
Dena Garson

Copyright © 2016 by Dena Garson
ISBN: 978-1-68361-018-2
Cover art by Fiona Jayde

Published by Decadent Publishing Company, LLC
Look for us online at:
www.decadentpublishing.com

Dedication

This one is dedicated to my boys—my greatest source of joy and frustration. My wish is that you always know you are loved more than you can possibly comprehend.

I also need to send out a big thank you to Rebecca R. and Virginia C. for getting me involved in the Black Hills Wolves! Hugz!! And to Hollie Neighbors for helping me wrap my head around the wild world of the Black Hills National Park and National Forest.

Chapter One

From the shadows of the surrounding foliage, Wyatt Powell watched the slip of a woman move about her campsite with ease. The business card she had left with the girls at the ranger office read, *Dr. Isabelle Acker, Wildlife Biologist.* It seemed, she was used to camping outdoors.

But even if she had been camping for over five years, it was damn foolish of her to be out here alone.

Normally, he wouldn't have paid much attention, but when he'd overheard the girls saying she was well known for her study of wolves, he'd been compelled to investigate.

Everyone knew there were no wolves in the Black Hills.

For generations, his pack had cultivated that belief. And in truth, there were no wolves. At least not what one would call a "normal" wolf. Wolf shifters were a whole other matter.

So, what brought Dr. Acker here?

She'd set up her camp in a secluded spot, well away from the established sites. Perhaps she wanted privacy. But for what?

The longer he watched, the more fascinated he became by her. It wasn't because she seemed at ease in the outdoors. Nor was it just a physical attraction. Sure, she was pretty for a human but not in a remarkable way. She was an average height with an athlete's build. Her plain brown hair had been pulled into a simple ponytail, but it did glitter a bit when she stepped into patches of sunlight.

Yet something about her had captured his interest. Both man and beast wanted to learn more.

He was about to retreat into the woods when he saw her gather a towel and a few bathing items and head to the nearby stream. His conscience argued he should leave and allow her some privacy, but the bulge behind his zipper insisted on following her.

Part of him wanted to know how much of a nature lover she was.

Like a deer, she picked her way over the rocks until she found a spot next to the river. Before sitting, she slowly turned her head in both directions scanning the area.

Wyatt had been taught by his Sioux grandfather the value of patience when tracking prey. Or a foe. Despite his base attraction, he had yet to determine which she might be.

Seemingly satisfied by what she saw or didn't see, Isabelle reached for her ponytail and pulled the band out. Her hair cascaded in waves down her back. Copper flecks became apparent now that the strands were no longer confined. She pushed her shorts off and then her denim shirt, leaving her in nothing but a tiny pair of panties and a white undershirt. Neither of which covered much.

He revised his earlier thought about her being unremarkable. The swell of her breasts beneath the clingy fabric made his mouth water. He lifted his nose into the air to catch her scent but picked up nothing except the expected foliage and damp earth.

Odd. Must be too far away. Satisfied no one else could see the treasures she had revealed, he adjusted his crotch to ease his discomfort and crept closer.

Sitting on the rock next to the stream, she looked as if she could have been in any bathroom in the world not the wild outdoors where dirt, bugs, and animals were the norm.

When she dipped her feet into the water, she jerked them away before easing them all the way in. Wyatt knew from experience the water in this part of the park would be chilled despite how hot it had been lately. Using her hand as a scoop, she rinsed her arms and legs. Next, she splashed water on her face and ran her hands through her hair. With her head bowed, she gazed into the water as if debating something.

Was she thinking of taking a swim? The stream was not deep, but the current was stronger than one would expect.

Before he could finish the thought, Isabelle hopped into the water.

Wyatt shot to his feet and ran to the river's edge to make sure she hadn't fallen on the rocks.

He scanned the surface of the water but didn't see her. When she came up for air, she reminded him of the Sirens Odysseus had faced on his voyage home.

Mesmerized, Wyatt froze. Even though he could only see her from the waist up, the blood in his head pounded and rushed south to his groin, leaving him off-kilter. Thankfully, her back was to him so, when she ducked under the water again, he had a chance to catch his breath and regain control over his raging hormones.

When she came up for air the second time, she faced him. Her eyes widened, and her mouth fell open at the sight of him standing on the bank overlooking the river. She sank lower into the water and narrowed her gaze.

"Do you realize you're polluting one of the park's water sources?" His voice came out far more steady than he felt.

She kept her body hidden beneath the waterline. "Not any more than a deer or bear that wanders into the water. I'm not using any soap or chemicals."

"Good thing. I'd hate to write you a ticket, Dr. Acker."

Her eyes narrowed. "And you are?"

He hopped down to a flat spot, level with the water's edge, then bent and stuck his hand out to her by way of greeting. "Wyatt Powell, park ranger."

She looked at his outstretched hand then into his eyes. "Nice to meet you, Ranger Powell. But if you don't mind, I think I'll stay right here."

He shrugged and stood upright. "Suit yourself." He stepped away from the water. "Nice day today. But I'm willing to bet that water's still pretty cold. It rarely gets above sixty, even by the end of the summer."

"That I believe," she mumbled. "Did you need something, Ranger Powell? Or do you make it a habit to drop in on park visitors at inconvenient times?"

The underlying sassiness in her tone appealed to him. "I do keep an eye on what goes on in the park. I understand you're a biologist," he said, switching topics.

"Yes, I am."

"Where are you from?"

"Georgia."

He nodded. "So, what brings you to our part of the

country?"

She shifted positions. Because she lay on her belly, he had a nice view of her backside despite the moving water. "I, uh...." She glanced at her clothes and towel on the bank not far away. "It's a little colder in here than I like. Do you mind if we finish this conversation at my campsite?"

He gestured to her things, pretending innocence of her predicament. "Sure. I'm in no rush."

"No, I mean...." She glared at him, then harrumphed and rose to her feet.

Wyatt's breath lodged in his chest when he saw her shapely figure through the T-shirt clinging to her skin. Her rosy nipples stood erect thanks to the cool water and shone like beacons through the almost transparent material.

She swept her hair to one side and twisted the water from it. When their eyes met, defiance flared like a candle. He had provoked her, but she met his challenge and raised the stakes.

When she took those few steps to the bank and reached for her towel, he had a perfect view of her backside. His growing erection forced him to rearrange his crotch. Giving any indication of how she affected him would do nothing but fuel the fire simmering between them.

He needed to keep his wits to determine how much of a threat she might be to the pack.

"Is that what people from Georgia swim in these days?" he called across the river.

She glanced over her shoulder as she wrapped the towel around her chest. "Only when we think we're alone and don't have a swimsuit."

"I don't believe you're ever completely alone out here," he cautioned.

She gave him another hostile glance as she pulled her shorts on. "Birds and wild animals don't count." Keeping her back to him, she pulled her wet shirt off and the dry one on. After gathering her things, she faced him. The smile she gave him appeared forced.

He chuckled.

"I feel the need for some coffee. Would you care to join me?" Her voice oozed exaggerated Southern charm.

Her challenge was too good to pass up. "Sure." They marched toward her campsite in silence until they reached the narrowest part of the river. There he crossed to her side and asked, "Is there something wrong with the public campsites?"

"No, why?"

"Most people prefer to be near the restrooms and showers, but you chose all the way out here. Why?"

"I want to see as much of the natural state of the park as possible. I can't do that around cleared areas filled with dozens of people. Especially when half of them have no respect for the environment."

"And you do," he said it as a statement, not a question.

"Yes."

"You know it's not safe for a woman to be out in the middle of nowhere. Alone."

She stopped. "Look. I heard enough arguments from my dad and my brother before I left. I am well aware of the risks." Her hand flailed as she spoke. "I've been hiking and camping for more years than I can remember. I'm in better shape than most men, and I've taken enough self-defense classes that I could teach them by now." Planting her hands on her hips she declared, "I can take care of myself."

He raised his brow. "I assumed you could. Otherwise, you wouldn't be here. But that doesn't mean it is without risk, and I am obligated to point it out."

"Fine." She resumed her march. "You pointed it out. Thanks."

Taking the lead in the conversation, she quizzed him about his background, his job, and how long he'd worked for the park. Wyatt had the feeling she was sizing him up for something. When they reached their destination, she waved him toward the chairs under her trailer's canopy.

"So, tell me. Have you noticed any environmental changes around the area?"

Wyatt frowned. "Like what?"

She flitted from her trailer to her table, gathering things for the coffee. "Climate changes, increased rainfall, more flowering plants, less bees. Anything that could impact the overall habitat of the region."

"That's kind of a broad question."

"Yeah, I know. Just wondering if anything stands out to you."

"Our weather hasn't been out of the ordinary. Like

everywhere, we've had years that were too dry and others where we had a problem with flooding." He scratched his jaw as he searched his memories. "Can't tell you whether there's more or less flowers around. There are few varieties I keep an eye out for. As for bees, we had a couple of scientists show up a few years ago to study them."

"Really?" She handed him a cup of warm, not hot, java, then sat in the other chair with her feet tucked beneath her.

It occurred to him her feet were bare. Unusual for a city girl. "They said they were documenting every species of bee in the region. If they missed any, I'd be surprised. Those guys were devoted to their cause."

"Do you remember who conducted the study?" Excitement rang in her voice.

He shook his head. "No, sorry. Not off the top of my head. But I think I still have one of their business cards at the office if you're interested."

"That would be great. Thanks."

"Is that why you're here? To study the environment? I thought you were some big wolf specialist?"

"Wolves are my specialty. They are interesting because I believe their behaviors, or more to the point, changes in their behavior patterns can be an indicator of changes in the environment."

"What do you mean?"

"They act as an early warning system if you know what to look for."

"So, what are you doing in the Black Hills? There aren't any wolves here," he challenged.

"I think there are," she said in a matter-of-fact tone.

He raised his brow to mock her words, but inside, an alarm went off. "I've worked in the park for over five years. I've lived in the area my entire life. There are no wolves here."

She shrugged her shoulder. "I aim to prove that one way or the other."

Wyatt gulped the last of his coffee and stood. "Well, I hope you don't leave too disappointed."

"We'll see," she said with a sly smile.

"Thank you for the coffee." He set the cup on the table. "I need to return to work."

"So, was this a social call then?"

"Maybe a little of both." He pulled a business card out of his wallet and slid it under the mug. "That's my number. If you run into any problems, give me a call."

"Thank you."

He tugged the brim of his cap. "Be careful out here."

"I will."

With one last look, he headed to his truck. He hated the idea of her staying out here alone. She may have years of experience camping and be able to defend herself in many cases, but a lone female in the middle of nowhere was asking for trouble. Anything could happen.

But it wasn't his place to tell her otherwise.

Right now, his concern for the pack took priority. Her stay in the park could endanger the secrecy and privacy they'd worked so hard to cultivate.

Drew, their Alpha, would never allow that.

What would Drew do to her if he decided she was a threat? After some of the vicious things his dad had done, pack leadership still made him leery. But it would be worse if Wyatt didn't report what he knew and things spiraled out of control. Many lives—many families—could be affected, and that he couldn't live with.

As soon as he got in and buckled his seatbelt, he pulled out his phone. His call connected. "It's Wyatt. We may have a problem."

Chapter Two

Breakfast was a simple fare of coffee, dried fruit, and cereal. Isabelle rolled the limited information she had around in her head. She needed to charge her laptop battery. It had enough power to record her day's notes, but that would be about it.

If the clouds stayed at bay, she'd look for a sunny spot where she could leave her solar unit.

As she ran through her list of things she wanted to do for the day, she noticed an odd silence had fallen. She looked as deep as she could into the trees surrounding her. When her trailer wobbled unexpectedly, she set her bowl on the ground and rose to her feet.

The sound of snorting and snuffling drew her

attention. When she stepped around the corner of her trailer, she found a bear pawing at the cooler holding her perishable food. It was a large enough specimen that she didn't want to chance an entanglement.

She backed up, trying to make as little sound as possible. As she crept past the table, she grabbed her cell phone and laptop. She slipped the electronics into her backpack and pulled the strap over her shoulder. She scanned the trees for a suitable host as she slipped away.

At least she still wore her boots from when she had foraged for wood for the fire. It would have been difficult to scale a tree in her socks. She groaned knowing her legs were going to get scratched since her shorts weren't long enough to provide much protection from the bark.

She could probably make it to her Jeep without the bear noticing, but she didn't want to miss an opportunity to study it. The tree she picked should keep her out of the bear's line of sight but still allow her to see what it did. She climbed onto a limb sturdy enough to hold her weight, then slipped her pack off and secured it to a nearby branch. Despite the bark and various knots, she found a reasonably comfortable spot. From where she sat, she had a good view of her campsite.

The bear managed to get the cooler open and ate pretty much everything inside. As it struggled with the cooler, it knocked one of the canopy support rods loose and bent another. It had just turned its attention to the contents of the trailer when Isabelle heard a voice from below.

"You have a visitor."

Her tummy did that strange fluttery thing again upon seeing Ranger Powell below her. "I do."

"I'm guessing it isn't a welcome visitor?"

"Part of me is curious to see what else it will do, but most of me is annoyed I'll have to reset my camp and go shopping for supplies."

He looked up. "You want me to run it off?"

"How do you plan to do that?"

He shrugged. "I have my ways."

She frowned. "You're not going to hurt it, are you?"

"Only if she doesn't cooperate or gets out of control." He headed toward the bear.

Isabelle held her breath as she watched.

Ranger Powell pulled something from his belt as he circled the creature. He seemed to be speaking to it, but she didn't understand what he said. There were a few growls, but Isabelle couldn't tell which of them made the sounds.

The two of them danced just out of reach of each other, until finally, the bear ambled off into the brush.

"You can come down," the sexy Ranger said. "I doubt she'll be back."

"Are you sure?" Isabelle looked at the place where the bear had disappeared, waiting to see if it returned.

"Pretty sure."

"What did you say to it?"

"Say?" He moved closer to the tree.

"Yeah. It sounded like you were talking to the bear. What did you say?"

"The same thing you'd say to a stray dog if it were in your yard. I told her to move along."

"It didn't sound like English," she pointed out.

"It wasn't."

"Then what was it?"

He looked up at her with a half grin. "Are you always this persistent?"

"Usually. So, what language was it?"

"Sioux."

"Really?"

"Afraid so." He motioned for her to come down. "Toss me your bag, and I'll help you get down."

She let her backpack fall into his outstretched hands. He set it on the ground a couple of feet away then held his hands up as if waiting for her to drop into them. Yeah, that wasn't going to happen.

She turned and laid her belly over the branch, and then she swung down so she hung from her hands. The drop to the ground wasn't far, but Ranger Powell steadied her when she landed.

"Are you all right?" His nearness sent a fission of awareness zinging through her body.

"I, uh...yeah." She wiped her hands on her shorts to knock the bark off. "Thanks."

"You were smart to climb the tree. A lot of people panic and try to scare bears off by doing something stupid like banging on pots and pans. That backfires more than it helps. So, good thinking, Dr. Acker."

"Thanks." She slung her backpack over her shoulder. "And just call me Isabelle. Save the doctor stuff for the guy who gives you your tetanus shot." With a grimace she went to see how much damage the bear had caused. "Just so you know, scientific curiosity outweighed any smarts. I wanted to see what the bear was after and what it would do."

He frowned. "Please tell me you didn't leave food out hoping to attract animals."

She stopped and glared at him. "What kind of idiot do you take me for?"

"You tell me. You said you wanted to see what it would do."

"Yeah, but that doesn't mean I tried to attract the bear's attention." She put her fist on her hip. "Or any animal's for that matter."

"Wouldn't be the first time a tourist did something stupid like that."

"I'm not a tourist. And I'm not stupid. Thank you very much." She stomped over to her trailer to see what could be salvaged.

The bear had bent one of the poles but it wouldn't

take much effort to bend it back into shape.

She walked to the backside of the trailer. Her cooler was another matter. It had been scratched and the lid was half torn off and filthy. There would be no salvaging that. Even if she managed to scrub it clean, the lid would probably never seal.

With a sigh she said, "Guess I need to go shopping."

"There are a couple of convenience stores nearby, but if you want to replace this stuff"—he pointed to the mauled items—"you'll need to go into town."

"How far is that?"

"Not quite an hour away." He tugged on his ear. "Now if you want a big-name place, you'll be better off going into Rapid City."

She groaned. "That's one way to kill an entire day."

"At least you weren't hurt."

"True." She faced him. "Thank you for chasing the bear away, Ranger Powell."

"You're welcome. But if I'm supposed to call you Isabelle, you need to call me Wyatt."

"All right." She wagged a finger at him. "If we're going to be friends now then I feel comfortable saying you shouldn't have taken such a foolish risk.".

He shook his head. "You could have stopped at thank you."

"True. But I'm willing to bet there are very few people who tell you when you're being a butt head."

"A butt head? How was I being a butt head?" His eyes were wide with shock.

She crossed her arms over her chest. "By confronting that bear unarmed."

"Who said I was unarmed?" he grumbled.

"I don't see a shotgun on you."

He pulled a small gun-like device out of his belt. "I had this."

She looked into his outstretched hand. "What is that? A Nerf gun?"

"It's a Taser."

"Like what the police use? Wouldn't a Taser just make the bear mad?"

He chuckled. "A normal Taser, yes. Mine is designed for wildlife. It packs a much bigger punch."

"I didn't know such a thing existed."

"I'm surprised. You've spent time in the field. Surely some of your colleagues have something similar."

"Mavis carried a Taser, but hers looked like an oversized lighter."

"Those wouldn't do you much good against a bear."

"I wouldn't think so," she mumbled as she resumed her search for undamaged supplies.

"Do you need any help?"

"I haven't looked close enough yet, but I may need help with those poles."

"All right. Let's see how bad it is."

They worked together pulling her things out of the way and disassembled the supports the bear had fallen against. Surprisingly, Wyatt was rather helpful. A little bossy. But no worse than her brother.

Each time she brushed up against him, a ripple of electricity zinged through her body.

By the time they finished, her panties were damp and she barely had a leash on her need to explore his tonsils with her tongue. At least they'd managed to return her canopy to its rightful place.

She put a bit of distance between them. "Once again, I appear to be in your debt."

"I'll tell you how you can repay me."

She lifted her brow in question, "How's that?"

He grinned. "I'm a sucker for hobo breakfast casserole."

That was not what she expected to hear. Disappointment trickled through her. "Really?"

He stepped close. "It's been a while since I've had any, though. What about you?"

She blinked and tried to focus on what he'd said. "Uh, same here."

"So, what do you say? Breakfast tomorrow?"

"Um, sure. I could do that." Butterflies flitted around in her belly.

His smile grew. "Excellent. How about if I bring juice?"

"Okay."

His amber eyes reminded her of aged bourbon.

Before she knew what was happening, she leaned into him. Their lips met, and her senses went on overload. He tasted minty with a hint of coffee. She melted against him.

His hand slid up her spine and pulled her closer. Tipping his head, he deepened the kiss.

Isabelle whimpered. She'd never been kissed so thoroughly. Even her toes tingled. She gripped the front of his shirt in a desperate attempt to ground herself.

When he pulled away, it took a moment for her eyes to focus. Wyatt watched her with a curious expression on his face.

"I, uh...." She bit her lip.

"I should probably go," he said gruffly.

She nodded.

Still he didn't release her. "You need to get to the store."

She blinked, unable to find any words.

"I need to check a few other campsites."

"Okay," she said.

Finally, he took a step back. "Do you think you can find your way to Rapid City, or do you need directions?"

"I, uh, I have a GPS."

"Good." He gave her a look that could have melted butter in the middle of winter. "See you in the morning, then."

"Yes. Tomorrow."

He turned and sauntered into the trees. She watched until he disappeared then turned her attention to the mess the bear had left behind.

She took a steading breath.

Hoo boy. That kiss would be staying with her for a while.

Perhaps the last few months of celibacy had not been a good idea. Here she was, ready to wrestle the first guy who kissed her to the ground and strip his clothes off.

She fanned herself and focused on what she needed to do.

Yes. Focus.

Trash bags. She needed to buy trash bags from the store.

Chapter Three

Wyatt's meeting with Drew went as expected. He wanted Isabelle watched. Closely. Two of the younger pack members would be enlisted to make her stay "uncomfortable." Nothing overt. Nothing dangerous, but definitely annoying. And Drew wanted as much information about her as Wyatt could gather.

In short, Wyatt needed to cozy up to her and find out what she was doing, what information she might be gathering and why. Drew also wanted to be notified the minute it became clear she presented a threat to the pack.

This morning's breakfast would be the perfect opportunity to learn what he could.

He parked next to her Jeep, then got out and

listened to everything around him. It was a habit. Nature told a great many things, but most people didn't take the time to listen. In this case, all appeared well.

As he neared her trailer, the smell of breakfast sausage greeted him. Isabelle sat at her table, working on her laptop.

"Good morning," he called, so he wouldn't startle her.

She looked up from her computer. "Good morning."

The smile she gave him made his heart skip a beat. "Are you working or playing this morning?" He indicated her laptop with a dip of his head.

"Actually, neither. I keep a journal." She wrinkled her nose. "Kind of old-fashioned but it helps me sort through things, and it acts as a log in case I need to remember details of my work. So I guess it's part personal and part work." She closed the lid and set the device aside. "How are you this morning?"

"Good. Thank you." He held up the jug he carried. "I brought juice."

"Oh, good. Thanks." She pointed to the other end

of the table. "Just set it over there. Coffee is ready so help yourself."

"You seem to be in a good mood. Did you have an exciting evening?" Even as the words left his mouth, the implication struck him. His Wolf growled at the thought that she may not have spent the night alone.

"Well kind of. I went for a walk after I returned from my shopping trip, and I stumbled across a small herd of antelope. Fortunately, I saw them soon enough and hid so I could study them for a while. But something startled them and they took off. Very exciting though. We don't have antelope in Georgia."

He smiled, understanding her excitement. "We have a herd of buffalo also. Did you know that?"

She stood and motioned him toward the campfire. There were two blankets on the ground next to the fire, and he noticed she'd cooked their meal over an open flame. Impressive.

"I had read there were some." She tilted her head. "Where can they usually be found?"

"There's a section of land northeast of here where they roam. A friend of mine also owns a ranch and raises them. He has one of the largest herds in the state. I can take you up there if you'd like."

"Don't you have to work?"

He shrugged and took a seat where she had indicated. "Yeah, but part of my job requires me to check in with the people who work with the animals and make sure everything's all right. I haven't checked on George in a few weeks."

"Is that your friend with the ranch?" She sat on the blanket next to him.

"Yes. He also coordinates the buffalo roundup they have when the herd gets too big."

"How many do they have?" She reached for the lid on the skillet.

"I'm not certain anymore. Used to be over a thousand head."

"I don't want to take you away from your duties, but I would love to see the buffalo and have a chance to talk to some of the people who work with them."

"It wouldn't be a problem."

With a smile, she exclaimed, "Great." She used her oversized spoon to check the food on the bottom of the pan. "I think breakfast is done. Hope you're hungry because I can't eat all of this."

The familiar aroma of campfire breakfast wafted across to him, and his stomach rumbled.

Isabelle grinned. "I guess you are." She scooped a large portion onto a plate and passed it to him. "There's some canned fruit on the table if you want it."

"Would you like some juice while I'm up?"

"Yes, please. And would you mind grabbing a couple of forks?" she asked as she ladled food onto her own plate.

"Sure."

When he returned, they dug into the casserole with relish.

"This is delicious," he told her between bites.

"Thanks. It's been a while since I made it. It's usually just me and my lab partner when I stay out in the field. But she's a health nut who would rather have a handful of granola than real food." She shook her head.

Thanks to the research he'd done on the Internet he had enough of her background to quiz her about her studies and the last paper she'd published. He may not have a PhD, but he could speak her lingo. As it turned out, they had a lot of common interests. He was tempted to bring up politics in order to see how compatible they were, but courtesy won out. Instead, he turned the conversation to sports. She surprised him by her enthusiastic support of one of the professional football teams.

He became so caught up in their banter he almost missed the twins sneaking through the brush. Keeping his expression neutral, he tried to figure out what they were up to. Drew must have ordered them to cause trouble for Isabelle. The twins were well known in the pack for pranks. Normally, they were just mischievous, but out here, things could go wrong in a big hurry.

It may be best to stick around for a little longer.

As he quizzed Isabelle about her hopes for the Super Bowl, he kept an eye out for trouble.

Soon a low rumble echoed in the distance. The rumble turned into a vibration in the ground.

"What is—"

Wyatt dropped his cup and yanked Isabelle to her feet, cutting off her question. She didn't resist and allowed him to pull her to the nearby cluster of trees.

Using the trees as cover, he wrapped his arms around her and pinned her in place.

Barely a second had passed before a large herd of elk trampled their way through the camp. He cringed knowing she would have a few more things to replace after this "accident."

The ground shook from the force of galloping hooves while limbs snapped and cracked as debris fell from the trees. Many of the lower branches were pulled off in the animals' haste to get by.

Damn twins.

Drew said to make Isabelle's stay uncomfortable, not attempt to kill her. He couldn't imagine how they'd managed to drive the herd through this narrow spot, but he planned to have words with them later.

As soon as the herd had passed and he believed it to be safe, Wyatt leaned back and looked down at the tiny woman in his arms. She hadn't panicked and, even now, only appeared somewhat shaken. "Are you okay?"

Her eyes were a bit dazed. "I, uh...." She licked her lips. "Yeah. I think so."

The sight of her pink tongue sliding across her lips

captivated him. Not caring about the consequences, he slowly lowered his head and touched his mouth to hers. Tasting. Testing.

Her breath hitched and she stilled, but in a matter of seconds she responded. Her body curled into his. She skimmed her hands up his sides and chest then circled them around his neck.

His body tightened in response. He deepened their kiss, encouraging her to open to him. She responded with fervor, sending him up in flames.

Like a starving man, he grasped her ass and pulled her closer. When that wasn't enough, he hiked her leg up, encouraging her to wrap them around his waist so he could grind against her. Still he needed more.

He needed her. His Wolf was awake and hungry.

The thin T-shirt she wore became an annoying barrier. He pushed it and her sports bra up then palmed her breast. It fit his hand as if made for him. She gasped when his thumb flickered over the hardened nipple.

He tore his mouth away from hers and buried his face into her neck, fighting for some semblance of control. Her scent washed through him, making him even harder. He nipped her neck then pulled her up so he could latch onto her exposed breast.

Her fingers slid through his hair and held him in place. She made faint panting sounds that drove him mad. He pushed the rest of her bra out of the way so he could feast on the other breast. Isabelle clung to him as she ground her pelvis against his stomach.

Stepping back, he gave her room to ease down his body and stand on her own feet and then once again captured her lips. With a flick of his wrist, he unhooked the button of her shorts and pushed them over her hips until they slid down on their own. He traced his fingers over her belly and the tiny patch of hair at her juncture and then into her dampened heat.

She was wet for him. His Wolf growled in satisfaction.

Using the tip of his finger, he found the tiny bud he knew would drive her wild and made circles over and around it. She whimpered against his lips and clung to his shoulders. Her nails sank into his skin, heightening his awareness of her every move.

He worked her clit until the smell of her arousal

wafted up to him. The sweet nectar called to him. Breaking their kiss, he squatted before her and pushed her against the tree for support. He spread her legs, then pulled one over his shoulder to better access her core. As he held her gaze, he gave her a long lick across her now exposed center.

Her lips parted on a gasp.

With relish, he dove into her sweet heat. He licked and teased her clit and swirled his tongue around her opening. The back and forth brushes over the sensitive bud drove her higher and higher until her eyes closed and her head drooped backward.

When he latched onto her clit and suckled, she whimpered and tried to pull him closer. He slipped a finger into her channel and sped up the flicks across her clit. She ground against his face then gave one last cry as she came.

He steadied her against the tree as she rode out her orgasm. He lapped up her juices, memorizing her taste and scent despite his body's need for release.

As soon as he sensed she neared the end of her ride, he stood and pulled her against him. Her eyes were closed but still she reached for him. He tilted her head and descended upon her lips.

She fumbled with the closure of his jeans and quickly freed him. With the first grip of her hand around his erection, he struggled for control. He wanted inside her. He needed her *now*.

Against her lips, he murmured, "Condom. Wallet."

She nodded but didn't release her grip. Her free hand circled around to his pocket, and she pulled out his wallet. She handed it to him then dropped to her knees.

Wyatt's eyes almost crossed when her lips wrapped around the head of his cock. When her tongue traced circles down the sensitive line along the front side he stopped breathing. Knowing he wouldn't be able to take much of her exquisite torture, he dug for the condom he always carried with him then dropped the wallet to the ground. Using his teeth, he tore the package open then reached for Isabelle so he could stop her torment.

He rolled the thin membrane into place and then pulled her against him. His lips slammed into hers, and he devoured her. She responded with increasing passion. Her desire seemed unaffected by her orgasm.

"Hold on," he growled as he wrapped her legs around his waist and pinned her against the tree.

She swiveled her hips, centering herself over his stiff cock. As soon as her body opened to his invasion, he drove in deep. Her warm channel gripped him as she clung to his shoulders.

"Oh God," she moaned onto his neck.

Oh God was right. His Wolf wanted out. It wanted to claim her in a very primitive way.

Her tight heat quivered around him as he slid most of the way out and slowly sank into her depths again. He held her in place despite her attempts. She panted faster, and both of their hearts hammered against their chests.

When her body went rigid with tension, he loosened his restraint. He slammed into her over and over. His lips crushed hers, and they fought for air and the next kiss. When she bowed up tiny spasms rippled over his cock, shredding his control. He rode her until his world exploded, leaving nothing but the two of them.

He wasn't sure how long they stood there, each of

them gasping for breath, but when he had two brain cells to rub together, he realized she remained pinned between his chest and the tree.

"Can you stand?" he asked.

She chuckled. "Maybe. I'm not sure."

He withdrew from her body and gave her room to put her feet down. Keeping his hand around her waist, he made sure she was steady on her feet. "You okay?"

"Yeah." She pushed her hair away from her face and grinned. "What about you?"

"Other than the fact that I came so hard I'm seeing stars, I'm great."

She giggled. "That was pretty intense, wasn't it?"

"I'd say so." He dropped a kiss on her lips, then stepped back so they could each straighten their clothes. Leaving the condom on the ground next to the cluster of trees, he assured Isabelle, "I'll get something to put that in."

Her cheeks turned pink. "I may have a grocery sack you can use."

He found his wallet and made sure nothing had fallen out during his hasty exploration. After brushing his clothes off, he turned to see if Isabelle needed any help.

She finished buttoning her shorts and looked up. Their eyes met, and something sparked between them. The realization he wanted her again, right here and right now, boggled his mind. Her pupils dilated, and she bit her lip.

"I, ah...."

"We should...." They said at the same time and then laughed.

"I'll help you check your camp to make sure the elk didn't do any damage."

"That'd be great." She smiled.

What was it about her smile that made his pulse jump?

He needed to put some distance between them so he could think.

They checked the campsite but, other than the table being knocked over, only a can of fruit had been damaged. Everything else was just scattered and dirty. Even her laptop had been spared.

"I should head to the park office. I'd like to check the area to see if I can figure out what triggered the herd to run like that."

"Let me know what you find out. And don't worry about this." She gestured to the mess around them. "Nothing was damaged."

"I'm glad, but I need to find out if there is a predator we're unaware of."

"I suppose that is part of your job, huh?"

Without giving her time to rethink anything, he swept in and gave her a very thorough kiss. Enough to leave his own lips tingling. "I'll check on you later. But call me if you have any more problems."

The dazed look on her face pleased him.

"Okay," she murmured.

He released her before he gave into the temptation to drag her into her trailer for the rest of the day. The supports under the mattress probably wouldn't hold up to the strain if he did.

On the way to his truck, he sacked up the used condom so he could dispose of it at the first available trash can. Instead of heading to the park office, he turned north so he could search for the twins. He needed to have a talk with them before they went too far.

Chapter Four

Isabelle stomped around her camp, fussing about wild animals. But every five minutes, her mind flitted back to Wyatt.

What the hell had come over her? He was good-looking, intelligent, loved animals as much as she did, and yes, his jeans did fit his ass just right. But she looked for more qualities than that in men she dated, much less slept with.

Granted, he had saved her from being trampled. And he did chase off the bear.

But they hadn't even been out on a date!

The sex had been off the charts, though. She couldn't remember ever letting loose like that. She always maintained an awareness of her surroundings. With Wyatt, she had surrendered to the moment.

She huffed her bangs away from her face and gathered up the things that needed to be washed.

It was odd to have so many animal problems. Normally when she camped, wildlife avoided her area. She allowed herself until noon to clean and put her camp to rights and then grabbed a quick lunch. After locking her laptop in her Jeep, she set out to explore.

The beauty of the area and the weather made her trek ideal. Warm, but not blistering hot. The variation in the landscape made her think she could stay a month and not get bored with the views.

Surprisingly, though, she hadn't found any evidence of wolves in the area even though her tracking software said one had come here from Georgia. Then again, anything could have happened to the chip she had implanted in the wolf to make it stop working. She just prayed nothing had happened to the wolf.

When she returned later that afternoon she found a note attached to her trailer from Wyatt.

Sorry I missed you when I came by. I had

planned to take you to see the buffalo, but I got pulled into a couple things and couldn't get away. To make up for it, I left a slice of homemade apple pie in your cooler. Sharon, one of the ladies in the park office, made it. You won't want to waste a crumb. Tomorrow should be a lighter day, so I could run you up to see the buffalo. And if you need a break from sandwiches and granola, I'll take you out for real food. I'll come by in the morning.

Wyatt

Isabelle's insides did somersaults. Part of her was annoyed he assumed she'd want to go. She did, and not just so she could have, as he put it, a real meal. Some of the butterflies in her belly were because she'd be seeing Wyatt. Knowing it was useless to stall, she went looking for his business card so she could send a text message accepting his offer.

She couldn't face him again without having a real shower. After grabbing her bathroom supplies, her hot water container, some clean underwear, and a towel, she climbed into her Jeep. The sun would set soon, and the showers would be busy around dinnertime, but she wasn't willing to pass up even a cold shower. Sure enough there were several people coming and going from the structure in the center of the camping area.

She made fast work of the cold water provided by the facilities and gave thanks she remembered to bring her solar-heated water bag for a couple of overall rinses.

Feeling a bit more refreshed, she returned to her trailer for a sandwich and fruit and then crawled onto her mattress and pulled out a book. The breeze blowing through the screens kept the temperature pleasant, but her light would attract far too many insects to allow her to sit outside and read.

Like earlier in the day, her mind strayed to Wyatt and their heated encounter. After rereading the same page three times, she set the book aside and turned out her lamp.

She was anxious to see him again even though she knew she wouldn't after this week. She needed to remember it was pointless to become attached.

But that didn't mean she couldn't enjoy the sex.

It was nice being away from men who were as

interested in her father—and in some cases, more—as they were in her. Out here, she was merely Isabelle. Not Scott Acker's daughter. Maybe that was the reason she had never met a man she could open up to.

Despite her mother's reassurances there was one man meant for her and she'd know him in an instant, she was losing hope of ever finding him. So, why shouldn't she enjoy Wyatt's company while she could?

With thoughts of all the naughty things she could do with Wyatt on the way to or during dinner dancing through her head, she fell into a restless sleep.

Sometime during the night, her dreams changed. She ran through field after field following something, but she couldn't see what. Fields turned into hills, then into rocky cliffs. Still she followed. The path led her to a cave at the top.

"Hello?" she shouted, her voice echoing off the cavern walls.

She made her way deeper into the cave until she found a large open chamber. It occurred to her she could see in the darkened passages but didn't.

Looking around the chamber, she noticed crystals in the walls emitting a pale blue light.

Off to the right, a dark figure moved. It crept forward until it became illuminated in the dim cavern.

The black form was a large wolf with dark fur and glowing amber eyes.

As it drew closer, a sense of familiarity washed over her. Somehow she knew this wolf.

She sank to her knees and ran her hands through his thick fur. He made low growls of approval and nudged her chin with his nose. When their eyes met, she knew she had found an old friend.

As she stared into its eyes, she felt herself being forced back to the real world.

She came awake with a start. Sitting up in bed, she clutched at the sheet wrapped around her and tried to gain her bearings.

The first rays of dawn lit the other end of her camper. Cool morning air filtered through the screens. There was a distinct smell to the first hours of the morning, and she breathed it in, trying to catch the smallest whiff.

Her sense of smell had been off ever since she had volunteered to take part in the testing of one of her mother's new drugs. As luck would have it, she had not been a placebo recipient. But it was a small price to pay if it meant helping hundreds. Maybe even thousands.

Over time, her mother hoped it would wear off and her sense of smell would return.

Pushing that thought aside, she focused on what she hoped the day would bring. Seeing the buffalo would be a treat. Having Wyatt as a tour guide would be a bonus.

What should she wear?

She hadn't packed any nice clothes. At the bottom of her bag, she found a pair of jeans she hadn't worn yet. There were a couple of clean T-shirts also. It may be a good time to break into her emergency concealer and mascara stashed in the glove box.

Each time Wyatt had seen her, she had been without makeup and a tad grungy, so today she wanted to look nice.

Before she forgot, she pulled out the clothes she wanted to wear and hung them over one of the canopy support beams. The breeze would shake a few wrinkles loose while she ate breakfast.

She went through her morning rituals. It took some time to brush all the tangles out of her hair and work it into a single braid so her breakfast had to be something quick and easy. After loading her pack with what she needed for the day, she then pulled out her laptop so she could work on her journal while she waited for Wyatt.

Her entry hadn't yet been saved when he arrived.

"Good morning," he called out.

She drank in the view of him in yet another pair of well-worn jeans and a T-shirt that fit him like a second skin. The rugged-ranger look was becoming one of her favorites. "Good morning to you. Coffee is ready if you want some."

"I filled up before I left the house. But thank you." He walked up to her, tipped her head backward, and dropped a leisurely kiss on her lips.

A slow sizzle began at the base of her spine and spread to all of her body parts. When he lifted his head, she could almost see sparks arcing between them.

She could kiss those lips for hours.

"Sleep well?" he murmured.

"I, uh...yes. Mostly." She shook herself free of the sensual haze he'd created. "How about you?"

"About the same." He straightened from his hunched position. "Are you anxious to see the buffalo? I assume you don't have any of those in Georgia either."

"No, we don't and yes, I am anxious."

"I thought we could get an early start, so you could see all you wanted before lunch."

She cocked her head to the side. "Are you sure you have time?"

"I wouldn't have offered if I didn't."

"I suppose that's true," she mumbled. "So, how are we going to get there?"

"We'll drive to George's stables and borrow a couple of four-wheelers." He narrowed his gaze at her. "Have you ever driven one before? I didn't think to ask beforehand."

She smiled. "I'm not an expert, but yes, I have driven one."

"Good."

Isabelle gathered her things and stood. "Let me change into my jeans, and I'll be ready to go."

"Need help with that?" he said with a boyish grin.

She gave him a sassy look over her shoulder. "Depends on how soon you planned to get to the stables."

He growled low in his throat. The sound sent chills down her spine and her extremities. She stopped at the door of her trailer and debated dragging him inside. It might be fun to waste an entire morning doing naughty things to each other. However, the scientist in her protested.

"Go get dressed. We'll have time later," he told her, reading her thoughts.

The smoldering look in his eye was almost her undoing despite his words. But she continued into the tiny space. She put her laptop away and grabbed her backpack along with a couple bottles of water. When she set those outside, she pulled her jeans off the beam where she'd left them and shook them out.

In less than a minute, she was dressed and working to secure the trailer. Wyatt helped with the latches then took her pack and led the way to his truck.

"You're not much of a talker, are you?" she asked as she climbed into the cab of his pickup.

"Not particularly, no." He started the ignition. "You're not one of those people who feels compelled to fill every minute with conversation, are you?"

She chuckled. "No."

"Good. Then we'll get along great." He managed to turn the truck around, despite all of the trees.

Once they were on the road, Isabelle drank in the scenery she had not been able to enjoy while she drove. The park had a wonderfully varied landscape that took her breath away. "It's beautiful here." She looked at Wyatt. "You're lucky to have a job that lets you see this"—she gestured to the window—"every day."

He shrugged. "It certainly has its moments. Good and bad."

"You could say that about any job though."

"I suppose."

"Did you tell me that you were from this area?"

"Yes. I grew up on a reservation east of here."

"Reservation, as in Native American land?"

"Yes." His tone went flat as if waiting for some kind of insult or criticism.

"I've never been on a reservation."

"I am not surprised."

"Did you like growing up there?"

The look on his face made her think he was surprised by her interest.

"I—" He turned his attention to the road. "Yes and no," he finally answered. "As a child I hated it. There was a lot of stigma attached to those of us who lived on tribal lands. Everyone thought we were poor and lazy. But after I left home and joined the Army, the things I had learned from my grandfather served me well, and I have a much greater appreciation for my heritage. And my home."

"Your grandfather is a Native American, I take it?"

"Yes. Full-blood Sioux."

"Is that your mother or your father's side?"

Once again he seemed surprised she had asked. "My mother's."

"If he has always lived within the tribe, I bet he has some interesting stories."

"Yes, he does," he murmured.

She returned to watching the scenery but couldn't help but add, "If someone hasn't done it already, you should write those stories down."

"Actually, some of the elders are working on that."

"Good. You should always know where you came from. No matter how ugly you may think it is."

She felt his gaze, but didn't look at him.

Her own history wasn't all that pretty, and to people outside her family, difficult to understand. One day, she hoped to have someone in her life that she could share all of those unpleasant details with. But until then, she'd keep them close to her chest.

"Would you mind telling me some of the stories your grandfather shared with you? I'm sure you have legends and myths and things."

He had enough time to tell her two short stories before they reached their destination. One about the Thunderbird and the other about the White Buffalo Calf Woman. Isabelle was charmed by them.

She was even more charmed by the man. He probably didn't realize it, but his entire demeanor relaxed as he recited the tales. She didn't think it possible for him to be more handsome than she already found him, but, in those moments, he was.

Chapter Five

Wyatt pulled into a gravel drive and parked not far from a large barnlike building.

"It's still a little early, so I'm not sure who's here," he confessed. "Would you mind waiting while I check at the office?"

"Sure, go right ahead."

Sure enough, he found Sarah in the main office bent over a newspaper with coffee in hand. Every time he saw her, he was struck by how much she resembled Reba McEntire.

"Good morning," he called out.

"Wyatt!" Sarah looked up from her paper. "What are you doing all the way out here?" She got up and greeted him with a hug.

"I have a couple things I wanted to run by George and get his opinion on. And I brought a friend along to see the buffalo."

"You're welcome to do both." She pulled him toward the door. "Let's go meet this friend of yours."

With little choice, he let Sarah lead him to the stables as she chatted the whole way. When they got close to the truck he motioned for Isabelle to get out.

"Isabelle, this is Sarah. She works for George." Wyatt smiled at Sarah. "Actually, Sarah is the brains of the operation. If anyone needs anything around here, they ask her, not George."

Sarah laughed. "That's because George can't stand being cooped up in an office." She nodded at Isabelle. "Just ask him. He'll tell you the same thing."

"It's nice to meet you," Isabelle said.

"George and Mackie are out checking on a calf that tangled with a bobcat or something a couple of nights ago. I'll unlock the door, so you two can take whatever you need." She raised a brow at Wyatt. "I assume you'll want a couple of ATVs?"

"You remembered." He'd never been able to ride a horse well. Every time he tried he had either worn himself out trying to control the animal, or he'd gotten thrown. George knew about his ability to shift. It was his theory that horses detected his wolf form, which made them skittish.

But Isabelle didn't need to know that.

They followed Sarah to a large door and waited while she opened the padlock.

"Everything should still be as you remember it," Sarah told Wyatt. "Gasoline is on the other side of the barn. Don't forget to fill them up when you return."

"George would never let me live it down if I didn't put it back the way I found it," he said.

"That's for sure," Sarah mumbled. "Okay. I'll leave you to it. But holler if you need anything."

"All right. We won't be out long," he assured Sarah. "And would you please tell George I need to talk to him?" he shouted after her.

She gave him a thumbs-up.

"Do you want an ATV of your own to ride, or would you rather be a passenger?" Wyatt asked Isabelle.

"Hmmm…. If I ride with you, I can pay more attention to the scenery instead of what I may be running over. But I do like speeding across an open area on one of these bad boys."

"Tell you what. You ride with me, and I'll let you drive it on the way back."

With a big grin she said, "Now that sounds like a plan."

George kept his machines in pristine condition. They picked a model that looked as if it would hold both of them. Wyatt pulled it from the building and then closed the door. He signaled for her to climb on.

Settling in behind him, she wrapped her arms around his waist.

Wyatt had second thoughts about her riding behind him. Her breasts pressed against his back and her hands so close to his crotch distracted him more than it should.

"So, how do you know George?" Isabelle shouted above the noise of the engine and wind.

"I used to work for him."

"Really?"

"Does that surprise you?"

"Honestly, no. But I am surprised I lucked into being able to hang with someone who knows the terrain and the animals well."

He grinned.

"What did you do when you worked here?" she prompted when he slowed down to cross a narrow stream.

"Everything from cleaning the stalls to repairing tack to leading trail rides."

"Sounds like you learned a lot."

"I did. George and my grandfather are the reason I finished high school. If not for them, there's a good chance I would have turned into another hard case and ended up in jail before I turned twenty-one."

"It's good that you had people like that in your life." She squeezed his waist, giving him a pseudo-hug.

"I owe them both a lot."

In the mirror, he saw a wealth of understanding in her eyes. How could the daughter of a wealthy businessman understand what a poor punk kid from the reservation went through? At least she didn't pity him. That he could never stand.

They passed several buffalo along the way, but he pushed on, looking for the herd. It wasn't long before they crested a hill and found hundreds of dark fuzzy beasts near a watering hole. He turned the engine off so it wouldn't disturb the animals.

A smile lit Isabelle's face. "Oh, my God. I didn't realize there would be so many of them. They're beautiful."

That made him chuckle. "No they aren't."

"Well, okay, they aren't pretty animals, but seeing them like this in their natural environment is wonderful!" She pulled a camera from her pack then slid off the seat. From a flat spot a few feet away she took several pictures.

He wasn't certain, but he thought she may have taken a couple of him. He shook his head. Must be a girl thing.

"I wish I could paint. That"—she gestured to the view before them—"would be awesome on a canvas hanging in my living room."

Their thoughts were eerily similar. He had photographs of some of the same views at his home. Unable to hold in his impulses any longer, he walked up behind her and wrapped his arms around her waist. With his chin resting on top of her head, he held her as they both drank in the view.

"Are you ready to head back?" he asked.

"Oh, I suppose," she said with a sigh.

He kissed her temple then gestured to the ATV. "You said you wanted to drive, so hop up front."

With a squeal of delight, she tucked her camera away and climbed onto the four-wheeler. She had to sit all the way at the front of the seat to reach the gearshift. When he sat behind her, he discovered some perks to being a passenger.

After showing her the gear positions and locations of the main buttons and levers, she drove the machine pretty well. He directed her to take a different route so he could show her places he'd always enjoyed. He didn't question why he had been compelled to share those with her. More than once in the last couple of days he'd wondered about his own behavior.

But her appreciation of those places made the effort worthwhile.

Not far from the stables, he directed her to a large open field where she could go as fast as she wanted and cut as many doughnuts as she dared without worrying about hitting an animal or tipping into any big holes. She giggled and whooped while he hung on for dear life.

Apparently, she had some daredevil tendencies.

His heart was racing by the time they returned to the corral. And it wasn't just from being one bump away from ripping her jeans off, turning her around on the seat, and impaling her on his now considerable erection. Every time she hit the gas, he rubbed against her butt cheeks. And his hands all but cradled her breasts as he held on.

With a sigh of relief, they parked near the stable and climbed off. Mackie came out to greet them.

Thankful for the distraction, Wyatt shook hands with him. "Mackie, it's good to see you. It's been a while."

"*Sí*. Too long, my friend." Mackie looked at Isabelle. "But if this is what's been keeping you away, I don't blame you a bit."

Isabelle's cheeks turned pink.

Wyatt chuckled. "Isabelle, this is Mackie. He's the best stable master around. Don't let him tell you any different."

Isabelle smiled and shook hands with Mackie. "It's nice to meet you. I don't know all that much about stables, but this one looks like it is run with precision."

Mackie tipped his head. "*Gracias*. Senor George is a good man. We all do our part to help." To Wyatt he added, "George said to tell you he'd be in his office and that you had better not leave without coming to see him."

"I'll go see him as soon as I've hosed off the four-wheeler."

"You don't need to do that." Mackie waved them aside. "You're a guest. Go. I'll take care of it."

"Are you kidding me?" Wyatt protested. "George would never let me live it down. But if you don't mind entertaining Isabelle, I'd appreciate it."

Mackie nodded. "*Sí*, how about if I show your lady friend around the stables?"

To Isabelle Wyatt said, "You're welcome to come with me and meet George. But I do have some official business to discuss with him."

"Oh, you go ahead. Besides, I'd love to see the horses." Her eyes sparkled with excitement.

"Well, I guess that's settled, then. I won't be long," he reassured them both.

He cleaned and refilled the ATV in record time, then parked it in the barn. When he realized he was all but running to the offices, he forced himself to slow down. As expected, he found George sitting at his oversized walnut desk, frowning at whatever stack of papers were in front of him. Wyatt rapped on the door frame to get his attention.

"Wyatt!" The giant blond-headed man stood and lumbered around to the end of the desk and reached for Wyatt's hand. With his other hand he pounded on Wyatt's back. "It's good to see you."

"You, too, George." Wyatt grinned. "How have you been?"

"Sit, sit." George waved him toward the chairs clustered on the other side of the office. "Other than this damned knee of mine, I've been good. What about you?"

"Fine. Just trying to keep the peace."

"Well, that can be difficult around here sometimes. But if anyone can do it, I'd put my money on you."

"Thank you. How's Shelly?"

"She's doing well. Still hounding me to retire and take her on a cruise to one of those islands out in the middle of the nowhere."

"Why don't you?"

"Bah." He made a scoffing motion. "Can you see me locked up in a room made for a dwarf while floating on the ocean for a week?"

Wyatt chuckled at the image. "Not really, no."

"There you have it." George rubbed his knee. "So, what brings you all the way out here?"

Wyatt told him about the two issues he wanted to discuss. First park business, then a land and cattle dispute one of his tribal elders had. George always gave logical advice, and Wyatt knew he'd be a good sounding board.

With a few sage words and a new perspective, Wyatt knew how to handle both.

"Now, I gotta ask." George leaned forward in his chair. "What did you leave outside that is so important that you feel the need to look out the window every other minute?"

"What?"

George stood and walked to the window. "You got a new truck and you're afraid someone will come along and steal it?" He looked at Wyatt. "This isn't the city you know."

"No. No new truck."

"Then what has you so anxious?"

"I'm not anxious," Wyatt denied. "I brought a friend with me. She's touring the stable with Mackie."

George whipped around. "She?"

Wyatt rolled his eyes. "Yes. She."

George hobbled over to his desk and grabbed his hat. "Well, come on. No need making a young lady wait while you and I gab." He opened the door and made shooing motions for Wyatt to precede him.

With a sigh, Wyatt did as his old mentor ordered.

"Now, tell me who this lady friend of yours is and how you two met."

"George, you're making a much bigger deal about this than is necessary. I just met Isabelle this week. She's here from Georgia doing research. I needed to come see you and offered to show her the buffalo. That's all there is to it."

"Uh-huh. I'll be the judge of that."

They found Isabelle and Mackie next to the stall at the end of the barn.

"What did you find?" Wyatt asked Isabelle when he saw her watching something in the stall with an expression of pure delight.

"It's a foal. Only a few hours old. Isn't he beautiful?" Her smile couldn't get any bigger if she tried.

The impact of that smile rocked him. He looked down at the infant and its mother. The foal was frail and wobbled like most newborns, but that didn't seem to matter to her. "Yes, he is," Wyatt said not about to disagree. "Isabelle, this is George. George, Isabelle."

She climbed off the rail and shook hands with George.

"I see Mackie is taking good care of you," George said.

"Yes, he is. You have a beautiful ranch, and I appreciate being able to see it." Her smile echoed in her voice.

They exchanged pleasantries as they all looked in on the mother and foal.

"So, what are you two going to do with the rest of your day?" George asked.

"I thought I'd take her to Ruby's Diner," Wyatt answered.

George nodded. "Excellent choice." He pointed his cane at them. "You better get going, or you'll miss out on the cobbler of the day."

Wyatt chuckled. "That's true. It was good to see you, George. You, too, Mackie. And thanks for letting us ride."

"Anytime." "You bet." George and Mackie spoke at the same time.

"It was nice meeting you both," Isabelle said with a wave.

"You, too, young lady," George said. "And if we don't see you again, have a safe trip home."

"Thank you," she called out.

They climbed into the truck and buckled up. As he pulled out of the gravel lot, she turned a smile on him that would have rivaled the sun.

"Thank you so much for bringing me out here. George and Mackie were very nice, and the ranch is wonderful." She reached across the span of the cab and touched his arm. "I had a good time."

"I'm glad. And you're welcome." He grinned. "But you've still got a treat coming. Ruby makes the best pot roast in the state. And her cobbler has won ribbons at the state fair."

"Oh?"

"I think we have enough time to get there before it sells out."

"Is that often a problem?"

"Every day."

"Really?"

He nodded. "Really."

They chatted about the history of George's ranch as they drove to Ruby's.

When they arrived, they found the parking lot full, as expected. He parked in the empty lot next door and helped her jump the small ravine separating the two lots. They had to wait a short while but, finally, two seats at the bar opened up.

As they reviewed the menu, Isabelle asked, "So, what's good?"

"Pretty much everything."

"That's what I was afraid of," she muttered.

He set his menu down. "I usually order based on how hungry I am."

"I'm pretty hungry." She looked at several of the tables around them. "Everything looks good. What are you getting?"

"I can't pass up her pot roast."

"That does sound good." She leaned closer. "If I get the barbecue brisket, would you mind if I stole a bite of yours? I promise I don't have cooties." The twinkle in her eyes drew him like a magnet.

"If you did, I think I'd have them by now," he whispered in her ear.

She laughed and pressed a kiss to his cheek. "I guess that's true."

The waitress brought two big glasses of water, took their orders, and then hurried off to help the next customer.

"I'm going to go to the bathroom to wash up. I've got a little more of the trail on me than I'd like when it comes to eating."

He nodded. "Good idea. They're in that far corner." He pointed her in the direction she needed to go.

Wyatt watched her weave her way through the crowded tables. Before she made it to the hallway, a tall, dark-headed man stood up from his table, blocking her path. The hair on Wyatt's neck prickled, and his lip curled when he recognized him.

Jaden was a Coyote shifter who had caused trouble for several members of Wyatt's pack. The fact that he was anywhere near Isabelle made his Wolf sit up and growl.

Jaden leaned close, making Isabelle lean away. The look of irritation she gave the guy was priceless.

Tension radiated through Wyatt's frame. If Jaden became foolish enough to lay a hand on her, he may rip both of the man's arms off and beat him with them.

With a furrowed brow, Jaden stared at Isabelle until she brushed past him. Then he locked gazes with Wyatt. Predictably, the guy headed in his direction.

"Your girlfriend isn't all that friendly," Jaden said by way of greeting.

"She is to me." Wyatt took a swig of the beer the waitress had brought when he wasn't looking.

"And she smells funny. What the fuck is wrong with her?"

"Nothing. Maybe that world-class sniffer of yours is off. Why do you care, Jaden?"

"I don't," he scoffed. "But something isn't right about her."

Wyatt shrugged. "I think you've been sniffing more than the local shrubbery. What are you doing here? I thought you were under orders to remain in your own territory."

"I've been checking in with some old friends."

"Didn't realize you had any," Wyatt observed.

"That's harsh, Hotah. I have friends. Just because we don't get along doesn't mean I'm the one with the problem."

"True. But you have a talent for pissing off everyone west of Rapid City."

Jaden gave them an evil grin. "It's a point of pride for me."

"Uh, Wyatt, is Mr. Doesn't-Know-the-Meaning-of-Personal-Space a friend of yours?" Isabelle asked when she returned. The look she gave Jaden made it clear she wasn't impressed.

Wyatt chuckled. "I've never called him that."

"Funny. Me either," Jaden said with exaggerated cheer.

Isabelle's brow rose.

Grudgingly, Wyatt made the introduction. "Isabelle this is Jaden. Jaden"—he gave the man a hard look—"was about to leave."

"It's true." Jaden shrugged. "I'm late for a meeting with my shrink."

Wyatt rolled his eyes.

"Well don't let us keep you." She brushed past Jaden and took her seat.

Jaden seemed surprised by her abrupt dismissal, which made Wyatt grin. "Give Stewart my best." Stewart was Jaden's pack leader.

"Sure." With a last look in Isabelle's direction, Jaden added, "Remember what I said. Something's fishy there." He tapped the side of his nose. "If I gave a shit, I might figure it out for myself, but since it's you...."

"Yeah. Thanks."

Wyatt watched until Jaden disappeared through the front door. What the hell was he talking about?

There was nothing wrong with how Isabelle smelled. Yeah, his nose twitched when he got close to her, but he dismissed it as a bad combination of bug spray and sunscreen.

But Drew needed to know Jaden had been sniffing around for some reason.

He sighed. One more thing to deal with.

Chapter Six

*D*ay Five: I've found no evidence of wolves in the area. While it is one of our nation's loveliest parks, and I've enjoyed seeing this part of the country, I worry my data may have been incorrect.

The visit to George's ranch, while unrelated to my research, was wonderful on a personal level. Once again the beauty of the land rendered me speechless. Seeing so much of it almost untouched gave me a sense of what it may have looked like hundreds of years ago. Wyatt lent personal insights to the ranch and how it came about, and he pointed out many things I may not have noticed on my own.

The time we've spent together was wonderful. Unfortunately, he received a distress call from a friend and had to leave not long after we returned. But he was nice enough to take the oversized snake we found curled up under the table away with him.

Despite spending years in the outdoors, I still don't like snakes. I need to remember to give Wyatt a suitable reward for taking care of yet ANOTHER issue for me. God, I'm beginning to feel like a helpless woman who needs rescuing. It's rather disturbing.

Isabelle finished making her entry in the journal then logged off her computer and put it away. She packed her satchel with the supplies she needed for her morning hike. Even if she couldn't find the wolf she had been looking for, she could still enjoy the scenery and study the animals that did inhabit the park. The weather couldn't be better if she'd planned it.

Her latest copy of the trail map went into the bag last.

Maybe today her camp wouldn't get raided by animals. Seriously. What were the odds? Five days in the park and four of them she'd had animal visitors.

At least none of her equipment had been damaged. Shredded and scattered paper she could deal with, but she was getting tired of eating canned food.

Normally, animals stayed away from her campsites.

Perhaps the local animals were far more used to park visitors than those at home.

She hadn't gotten far down the trail when she noticed a boy huddled under a tree. He leaned against the trunk with his knees pulled up to his chest and his head resting on his knees. If he hadn't been wearing a bright red windbreaker, she may not have seen him.

Slowing her pace, she checked the surrounding area for the boy's parents or a trail guide. Seeing no one else, she slowed and listened. Still, she couldn't tell if anyone accompanied the boy.

Unable to continue without knowing for sure, Isabelle headed toward him.

She kept her movements slow to avoid spooking the child. When she got close, she called out, "Hey, sport. Are you okay?"

He lifted his head and looked at her with heavy

eyelids. As he woke, he became alarmed and leaped to his feet.

Isabelle lifted her hands. "I only wanted to find out if you were all right."

The boy's lip trembled. "No."

"Are you lost?"

He nodded.

Poor thing. She took a few more steps toward him. "You weren't out here all night were you?"

Again, he nodded.

She closed the distance between them and touched his forehead. "Oh, sweetie. You must have been so scared."

"Uh-huh," he said with a whimper.

"What's your name?"

"Jimmie."

"Jimmie." She smiled, hoping to comfort him. "Are you hungry?"

He hesitated and then, in a small voice said, "A little."

She slipped her backpack off and placed it on the ground in front of her. "I have a fruit bar and some granola. You're welcome to have them."

His gaze darted to her bag then up to her face again.

Without waiting for him to answer, she fished the items out of her bag and handed them over. Next, she fished the extra bottle of water out, broke the seal on the lid, and handed it to him. Her heart ached at how fast he gulped down the first swallows. As he ate, she pulled out her phone.

"Are you gonna call my mom and dad?" he asked.

"No, honey. I would if I knew their phone number. I'm going to call a friend of mine. He's a park ranger. But if you know your mom or dad's phone number I will call them."

He shook his head. "Dad just got a new phone, and I haven't learned it yet." He sniffled. "Mom told me I should try to remember it."

She patted his shoulder. "It's okay. My friend will be able to help. Do you know what a park ranger is?"

"That's like a policeman, only for the park, right?"

Isabelle smiled, pleased he had at least heard of the term. "Yes. Kinda like that."

She dialed Wyatt's number. He answered within a couple of rings. "Dr. Acker. I hope you're calling because you missed me and not because you found another snake."

"No." She chuckled. "No more snakes but I do have something else I could use your help with."

"Not to be critical or anything, Izzy, but are you sure you're cut out for working outdoors? You don't seem to have much luck out there."

"Ha-ha. Very funny. No, actually, this time I've found something that you all should be interested in. His name is Jimmie and he is...." She looked down at Jimmie. "How old are you, Jimmie?"

"Eight."

"He's eight years old, and I believe he wondered off from his mom and dad sometime late yesterday."

Wyatt's voice became all business. "Where are you?"

She described the direction she had taken from her campsite and everything she could see around her as land markers.

"I'll be right there. Don't go anywhere." She heard the slam of his truck door through the phone.

"I didn't intend to," she reassured him.

"Is he hurt?"

"Amazingly enough, no. I don't think so."

"Thank God," he mumbled. "Okay. I need to call this in. Stay put."

"All right, Mr. Bossy Pants," she muttered, then disconnected the call.

"Was that your friend?" Jimmie asked.

"Yeah."

"Is he getting my mom and dad?"

"He said he needed call the park office. So my guess is they know who your mom and dad are."

"How are we going to get there?"

"My friend is going to come and get us."

Jimmie tilted his head to the side and furrowed his brow. "Will he be on a horse?"

"Er, no. He drives a truck."

"All the movies show rangers riding horses, but I haven't ridden one before."

"Well, I think they all drive trucks now."

He nodded.

"So, who did you come to the park with?" she asked. "Just your mom and dad?"

He nodded. "And my brother."

She held her hand out to lead him to the main

trail. "Is your brother older or younger?" She kept up her questions trying to both distract him and ascertain how he came to be lost in the woods all night.

It didn't take much to keep Jimmie chatting. Soon, she knew the name of his hamster, his favorite video game, and the book he had been reading with his mom.

At the sound of Wyatt's truck in the distance, Jimmie stopped and looked to Isabelle. "Do you think we should hide?"

"No. That should be my friend, the park ranger."

Jimmie's eyes grew worried.

"If it's not, don't worry, I'll deal with them."

Jimmie's shoulders slumped in relief.

Wyatt stopped a little way ahead of them. As usual, the sight of his muscular frame made her heart skip a beat. Her mouth watered at the sight of his tee stretched across his broad shoulders and chest.

As he approached, Wyatt looked down at the boy. "Are you Jimmie?"

The boy nodded.

"Your mom and dad have been worried about you.

Let's get you to the park office."

Jimmie looked to Isabelle.

"It's okay. He's a good guy," she told him.

"Will you come, too?" Jimmie's eyes conveyed his fears.

She glanced at Wyatt. "Sure."

Wyatt gently interrogated Jimmie as they drove to the office. Soon, the boy relaxed and volunteered information. When they pulled into the parking lot, Isabelle saw a woman waiting outside the office. The woman's expression was set in a worried frown, and she chewed on her sleeve.

"Mom!" Jimmie cried. Before Wyatt could put the truck in park, Jimmie reached for the door handle and tried to jump out.

The mother-son reunion brought tears to Isabelle's eyes. Jimmie's mom alternated between hugging him and checking him from head to toe. A man burst out of the office and joined them. Close on the man's heels came another boy. Soon, all four were caught in one embrace. Tears of relief and joy flowed freely.

"We've been looking for him all night. How did

you find him?" Wyatt asked.

Isabelle shrugged. "I happened to notice his red hood while I walked. He must have fallen asleep under that tree near the main trail."

"He doesn't appear to be injured."

She shook her head. "I don't think he is. I gave him a bottle of water and a fruit bar. He practically inhaled those, but he didn't limp or look like he had any scratches or bruises."

"He was lucky."

"Yes, he was," Isabelle agreed.

A park official came out and tried to herd Jimmie's family inside the office. Wyatt told Isabelle, "I best get in there also. If you wait a bit, I'll drive you to your campsite."

"Don't worry about it. I planned to take a hike this morning. I can take one of the other trails from here."

"Stay out of trouble," he told her. "I may have some questions for you later, so I can add your observations to the report. But right now, we'll focus on making sure Jimmie is taken care of and that there was no malicious intent." He looked over at the family. "But I think we can rule that out."

Isabelle nodded. "He seems like a good kid. I'm glad he's okay and that I could help."

"I'll give you a call later," he promised.

Isabelle admired the way Wyatt's jeans hugged his ass as he headed to the office. His T-shirt clung to his shoulders in a way that made her want to toss a glass of ice water on his chest so she could watch the drops run. All. The. Way. Down.

With visions of Wyatt's naked form in her head, she took to the trails to see what she could find in the wilderness.

Chapter Seven

Standing at a crossroads in the walking trails, Isabelle debated which way to go. As she often did, she wondered how early explorers got anywhere in the world and then home again. At least she had GPS and a number of gadgets at her fingertips.

It wasn't far to the tree line. From there, she wove her way through, taking her time and soaking in the sounds of nature. This was why she loved her job. She loved being in the middle of nowhere yet with so much around her.

She followed the trail of footprints and tufts of fur of what she believed to be a mature coyote for almost a mile before it led her farther off her path than she wanted to be. Just as she broke free of the tree line, she heard a gunshot. Curious why someone would be firing a weapon in a state park, she looked in the direction she believed it had come from. Now that the trees weren't blocking her view, she realized she had veered close to one of the main roads.

At the curve, there were two men arguing and gesturing between the nearby truck and whatever lay on the ground at their feet. A second look revealed a large set of antlers.

Outraged, Isabelle called out, "What did you do?"

When the men turned in her direction, she noticed the rifle hanging from the taller man's shoulder. She was so irritated by their thoughtlessness the fact they were armed didn't slow her down at all.

She gestured at the carcass. "Do you know what you've done?"

The man carrying the gun looked from her to the other man and back to her.

"That's a bull moose!" she declared. "And you shot it! How could you do that? I'm no expert, but I'm pretty sure that's illegal in a state park."

"Bob, I think we got us a busybody," the taller of the two said.

"I think you're right," the other muttered.

Isabelle continued her rant. "What do you have to say for yourselves?"

"At least she's pretty."

"Yeah, but the pretty ones are usually more trouble," the shorter man with the scruffy beard said.

"Trouble? It's the two of you who are in trouble. I'm sure the park rangers will have something to say about your target practice." She knelt next the moose and pressed her palm to its neck, then its chest but didn't feel a heartbeat. Her stomach sank.

How people could be so heartless?

Without warning, she was jerked to her feet by the shorter and, now that she was close to him, smelly man. "What the hell!" She tried to jerk her arm free but couldn't.

"You're coming with us."

She pulled against the short man's grip on her arm. "No, I'm not."

"Yes. You are." He tightened his grip and pulled upward, throwing her off balance.

"You're out of your mind if you think I'm going anywhere with the two of you," she told them.

"If you argue, you're just going to make him angry. Just get in the truck and nothing will happen to you. We'll drop you off somewhere along the way, and you can pretend you never saw us. Right, Bob?"

The shorter man growled in response.

"I don't think so." Isabelle yanked her arm free and turned to run for the woods. Before she could get away, the man named Bob tripped her and then used his body to pin her to the ground. The smell of his alcohol-drenched breath next her face made her stomach turn.

"Listen here. This here is our moose, and we ain't giving it up. We was just going to load it up in our truck and be gone, but now you're here, messing things up, and I can't let you do that. If you had minded your own business, no one would have ever noticed it missing. Now I got to figure out what to do with you."

"Get off me, you buffoon, before you end up getting hurt," she told him through clenched teeth. She struggled to remember which of them had the gun. What were her chances of flipping him off her and maybe even landing a punch or two without getting shot?

"I don't see where you're in any position to be telling me what to do," Bob said.

"Come on, man, let's get out of here. If we hurry, we can be out of here before anyone else comes. She don't know us, and she can't prove we did anything. If we let her go, maybe she'll promise to not say anything to anyone."

"Don't be an idiot," Bob snapped. "Of course she's going to tell on us. You heard her. She said the rangers were going to come after us."

"She didn't mean it, did you, lady?" the taller man implored.

Isabelle wished she could see the man's face so she knew whose hide he was more worried about, hers or his own. Something inside wouldn't let her lie to them. She knew if she promised not to tell on them, they might let her go, but the utter wrongness of the shooting prevented her from agreeing with him.

"See?" Bob crowed. "She can't promise. Go get the rope from behind my seat."

"Oh, man. Just let her go. We're already in a heap of trouble. I can't go back to jail. My old lady said she'd leave me if I did."

"Go get the dammed rope like I told you."

His fading footsteps and the squeak of a metal door hinge told Isabelle the other man had done as he had been told.

"Now, cut me off a section. I'm going to tie her hands."

Isabelle renewed her efforts to buck Bob off, but he was heavier than she expected. There was no way in hell she was letting them tie her up.

"I don't feel right about this," non-Bob muttered.

"Shut up and do as I tell you," Bob ordered.

Bob adjusted his weight then jerked her hand farther behind her back, making Isabelle gasp with pain. She bucked and twisted and struggled against his hold, trying to break free. She managed to get one hand free, but the blow to the side of her head made her ears ring and dots dance in front of her eyes.

"Aw, man, now why'd you have to go and do that?" non-Bob whined.

"That had better be your blood and not hers," a gravelly voice said from somewhere nearby.

Wyatt.

Bob twisted around but pressed his knee in the center of her back.

"Goddammit. I knew we was going to get busted," the tall man mumbled.

"You better stay right where you're at, or I'll cut her," Bob said.

Isabell stopped struggling when something sharp pressed against her cheek and ear.

"I suggest you put that knife away before I take it away from you. And I promise, you won't like what I do with it after that," Wyatt said with deadly calm.

"Now, Hotah, me and Bob was just leaving. We weren't going to hurt her or nothing. Just leave her somewhere that might take her a while to walk from."

Hotah? Did he mean Wyatt?

"You mean dump her in the middle of nowhere with no means of survival. Is that what you were thinking?"

Isabelle hadn't heard Wyatt take a step, but his voice sounded closer, and the tension in Bob's body had increased.

"Well, maybe a little like—" the taller man began.

"Will you shut up, Dalton?" Bob ordered. "Now

I'm serious, Ranger. Back off and we'll ease on out of here, and you can take care of the lady, and we'll all pretend like this never happened."

"I don't think so," Wyatt murmured.

Isabelle's emotions were a jumbled mess. Part of her was terrified. Another pissed as hell the stinky guy had her pinned to the ground. Yet another part was oddly turned on by the command that rang in Wyatt's voice.

"Looks to me like you're out numbered and"—the pressure of the knife against her neck lifted, and Bob's knee twisted on her spine—"I've got the knife *and* the gun. What you got, Ranger?"

"Me," Wyatt growled.

Suddenly, Bob was knocked aside, off her. The crack of fist against flesh made her scramble to her feet to help Wyatt. She found him straddling Bob, his fist raised, and then he landed yet another punch. Based on the blood seeping from Bob's nose and the limpness of his arms, another wouldn't be necessary.

The tall man took a step toward Wyatt and Bob, but froze when Wyatt snarled at him.

The hair on Isabelle's neck stood on end, and her

pussy clenched. *Holy cow!* What was it about Wyatt today? She had never had such an urge to rip someone's clothes off. Perhaps she had developed a thing for brawny men who came to her rescue.

"Wyatt? Can we get out of here?" Her voice was shakier than she intended.

His attention switched to her. His wild-eyed gaze held her enthralled, and, for a moment, she could have sworn his nose had grown and his eyes had darkened. She shook her head, and when she refocused, he looked normal.

Only much angrier.

He climbed off of Bob and wiped his knuckles on his jeans. "Dalton, you've got about two seconds to apologize to Isabelle for scaring her. Then you're going to help me toss your friend here"—he gestured to Bob's unconscious form—"into the bed of your truck. After that, we're going to head to the park office. Understood?"

Dalton's shoulders slumped in defeat. "Understood." He looked at Isabelle. "My apologies, miss. Bob don't usually mean no harm. I'm sure when he comes around, he'll be sorry, too."

Somehow she doubted that.

Wyatt frowned at Dalton then shook his head. "Help me toss him into the truck."

Together, the two of them lifted Bob, but Wyatt tossed the still-unconscious man into the metal bed of the truck without a hint of gentleness.

Wyatt pointed to Dalton. "You're ridding up front with me."

"What about me?" Isabelle demanded. *Unbelievable!* He hadn't said anything to her or asked if she was okay.

He tossed her a set of keys. "Follow us in my truck."

"Yes, sir," she grumbled.

On the drive to the park office, she called Wyatt several choice names. By the time she parked and got out, she had only released a fraction of her frustration but had come to the conclusion she wanted nothing more to do with the insensitive macho man even though he had an annoying habit of showing up in time to play the hero.

Wyatt led Dalton into the office with little more than a glance in her direction.

She rolled her eyes and followed them in.

When Isabelle entered, Sharon, the office manager she'd met earlier in the week rushed over and clasped her by the shoulders. "Are you all right?"

"I, uh...." She glanced at Wyatt. "Yeah. A little bruised, but otherwise, I'm fine."

Sharon pulled her into a hug. "Oh, you poor thing. That had to be terrifying." She released Isabelle from the crushing embrace but didn't let go of her. "Wyatt called us and told us what happened." She drew her toward an office at the rear of the building. "You come on back here while Wyatt deals with those two hoodlums."

"I wasn't planning on staying. I think I should go to my camp."

Sharon steered her into the office and pointed to the sofa against the wall. "No, no, no. You've had a bit of a shock. You need to sit right there and collect yourself." She patted Isabelle on the shoulder and didn't give her a chance to respond. "Besides, Wyatt may need you to answer some questions." Without stopping for a breath, Sharon continued, "Can I bring you anything? Water? Or a soda?" She didn't let

Isabelle answer before adding, "I'll get you an ice pack for your cheek." Sharon started to leave but stopped to say, "If you want to clean up, you're welcome to use the bathroom down the hall."

"Thank you." Isabelle managed to get a word in. "I should at least wash my hands and face."

"Well, you go right ahead. I'll bring you a bottle of water. We may have some canned fruit in the cabinet if you'd like."

"No, thank you. The water is all I need." Isabelle crinkled her nose and touched her cheek. It throbbed in time with her heartbeat. "Besides, I don't think I could eat anything right now."

Sharon nodded and made noises of sympathy. "Ah. I didn't think of that. Well, take your time. Wyatt may be a while."

Before Sharon finished her sentence, Wyatt appeared in the doorway. "Come on."

"Can your questions wait until I've washed up?" Isabelle groused.

"You can clean up in a bit. Let's go."

Isabelle looked at Sharon. She appeared confused by Wyatt's behavior but then smiled in Isabelle's direction. "Perhaps it would be best to get the questions out of the way while the answers are fresh in your mind."

Isabelle took a deep breath and resigned herself to putting up with Wyatt's questions and his bossy attitude. However, when she followed him to the front office, he didn't stop and, instead, held the door open for her to precede him.

"Where are we—"

"Just get in the truck."

"But—"

"Get in the truck, Isabelle. Now."

Despite the urge to tell him to kiss her entire ass, something warned her this was not the time to argue.

Without saying a word, she climbed into the passenger side and buckled her seatbelt.

Wyatt got in, started the ignition, and pulled out of the parking area without so much as a glance in her direction.

Finally, she had to ask, "Where are we going?"

"My place."

"Why?"

He didn't answer, just drove in silence.

Perhaps he needed to pick up something he'd left behind that morning and didn't want her getting in the way at the office. That was plausible.

After a few miles, they turned off the paved road. The turn would be easy to miss if you didn't know to look for it. When the trees opened into a clearing, she saw a simple yet contemporary ranch house. All of the wood siding lent a rustic feel to a modern structure, creating a unique combination.

Wyatt still said nothing as he parked and got out of the truck. Isabelle shook her head and followed him into the house. The living room had one wall of windows facing a small courtyard at the rear of the house. The leather couch and chair were set at perfect angles to the wall of books that also held a large TV. The entire area was much cleaner than she expected for bachelor quarters.

"Make yourself comfortable. I'll be back as soon as I finish some paperwork."

"You're leaving me here?" Her mouth hung open in disbelief.

"Yes."

Isabelle snapped her jaw shut. Through clenched

teeth she said, "I'm not staying here."

He took two steps in her direction. "Yes, you are. I have to finish filing charges on those two idiots, and I expect you to be here when I return."

With fists on her hips, she declared, "You have no right to tell me what to do."

He growled, "Don't push me right now, Izzy. You have no idea how much danger you were in. Dalton is an idiot and a follower, but Bob is cruel and dangerous, especially when he's been drinking. You could have been killed." His eyes turned dark gold. "Or worse."

She gulped. It had been foolish to confront the two of them. She hadn't allowed herself to think about how badly it could have gone.

A tremor went through her.

Wyatt pulled her into his arms. A little rough and a little too tight but she didn't mind. She sniffled back the tears threatening to spill.

"Now, listen to me. I have to go, but I need to be sure you are safe and that you'll be here when I return. Promise me."

She took a deep breath. "Fine." Some of the

tension left his frame, but he didn't relinquish his hold on her.

"Fine what?" he asked.

"Fine I'll wait here."

He grunted then kissed the top of her head and released her. He pointed to the hallway off to the right. "The bathroom is at the end of the hall. There are clean towels under the sink." He gestured to the other end of the house. "Help yourself to anything in the kitchen."

With a few steps, he returned to her touched her cheek with a feather like caress. "You need to put some ice on that." Then his face darkened, and he mumbled something about kicking someone in the nuts. Abruptly, he turned and headed to the front entrance. With one last look in her direction, he disappeared through the door.

When the latch clicked, her knees went weak. The reality of the day's events closed in on her. She clutched the edge of couch for support as she began to shake.

Breaking down into a weepy mess was not going to happen. She forbade it.

Perhaps a hot bath would help.

Using the wall for support, she made her way to the bathroom. She clicked on the light and was once again surprised. The room had a spa-like feel, thanks to its neutral colors and soft textures. In contrast to the décor, she found a soap dispenser shaped like a bright yellow rubber duck next to the faucet.

The rubber duck she found on the edge of the tub surprised her yet again. It was so out of place and cheerful her mood lightened instantly.

She couldn't stay mad at a guy who kept rubber ducks around.

After turning on the water and stopping the tub, she went in search of a towel. In the drawer below the sink, she found a razor that looked as if it had never been used. She could not turn down an opportunity to shave.

With a whisper of thanks, she took the shampoo and conditioner she found and headed to the tub. Putting all of her treasures on the edge, she sank into the steaming water.

It was going to feel so good to scrub every last inch of her body clean.

In a minute.

After the hot water relaxed all of her muscles and made the shakes stop.

She closed her eyes and reminded herself everything was fine. She was fine. Wyatt wouldn't have brought her here if it wasn't safe. Her gut said she could trust him. She just needed to relax and let the warm water do its job.

Chapter Eight

Wyatt returned home, anxious to see if Izzy had waited for him.

Those two jack-wads he had filed charges on were lucky. This close to the full moon, it had taken every drop of discipline his grandfather had taught him along with prayers to the spirits to not shift. If he had, his Wolf would have ripped the two of them to shreds.

Just thinking about what could have happened to Izzy set him on edge. If the mark on her face still looked as painful as it had before he left, he may be tempted to return to the office and inflict a little more damage on Bob. If he hadn't already come to the conclusion he and Isabelle were meant to be, his reaction would have proven it. His reaction had been too swift and powerful to be denied.

But how did he convince her to stay? And if he did, how would he break the news that once a month he had an uncontrollable need to run wild though the forest as one of the furry, four-legged beasts she had been studying?

He shook his head to clear it and got out of his truck.

His gut clenched. What if she wasn't there?

He unlocked the door and let himself in as quiet as possible.

A quick check confirmed the living room was empty and so was the kitchen. He padded down the hall.

The wet towel hanging over the shower-curtain rod told him she had taken a bath.

He hardened at the thought of her naked in his house.

When he stepped into his bedroom, his breath caught in his chest. She lay curled on her side in the middle of his bed, asleep. She had borrowed a T-shirt, but from his vantage point, he couldn't tell if she wore anything else.

He drank in the sight. His Wolf roared with a need to claim her.

Moving silently, he stripped out of his clothes and boots. Before climbing into bed with her, he grabbed a condom from the bedside table. He rolled the sheath in place then slid in next to her. His body molded to hers, causing her to murmur in her sleep.

He pressed his lips against the tender skin of her neck then down to her shoulder. When he nipped the muscle near her collarbone, she gasped.

"You're back," she said as she rolled to face him.

"And you're in my bed," he growled.

"I hope you don't min—"

He didn't give her a chance to finish. He devoured her lips as he pulled her tighter against him.

For a split second, he worried about being too aggressive. His Wolf demanded he take her, and his control had been stretched too far already today.

But she gave as good as she got.

Her kisses were a thing of dreams! The flicks of her tongue against his were part timid and part Siren. They teased and tantalized but were gentle enough to hint at her relative inexperience.

Her leg rode higher and wrapped around his hip. She sank her nails into his shoulder as she struggled to get closer. Her pussy rubbed against his erection, making Wyatt groan.

She was slick and ready for him.

He captured her hands and rolled her onto her back.

"I need you, Izzy. I can't be gentle with you," he said through gritted teeth.

"You don't have to be."

Taking that as permission, he pushed the shirt she wore up and wrapped it around her wrists. After pinning her hands against the pillows above her head, he buried himself in her heat.

Isabelle sucked in a breath at the invasion, but her pussy quivered around him.

He slid in, creating a delicious friction, but it wasn't enough. Deeper. He needed to fill her completely. He needed to mark her.

With gritted teeth, he withdrew from her body then flipped her onto her belly. He pulled her up onto her knees and positioned himself behind her. He drank in the sight of her rounded ass and curved spine. Unable to control himself for a single second longer, he grabbed her hip and aimed his cock at her opening.

With one thrust, and he was back in heaven. She squirmed and pushed against him, trying to impale herself upon him, but he kept a firm grip on her hips, denying her any leverage.

The mewing sounds she made in protest sent heat spiraling to his crotch.

He reached around her waist and found her clit. He teased the tiny bud with his finger, making her freeze. As soon as she responded to the stimulation, he renewed his thrusts. He felt the familiar tingle in his balls and knew he was close. As he struggled to hold off, he nipped her shoulder.

Isabelle threw her head backward and cried, "Oh!"

The quivering of her pussy around him was the final straw. Thunder roared in his ears as he came with blinding intensity.

He collapsed onto his side and pulled Isabelle's back against him, burying his face in her neck. At least he'd had the wherewithal to not fall on top of her.

He took a deep breath and drank in her scent. Despite being sated, his Wolf stirred beneath the surface.

Isabelle stretched and turned in his arms to face him. She grinned and gave him a gentle kiss.

Something fluttered in Wyatt's gut.

"Do you always come home from the office like that?" she asked.

"No. I suspect it had something to do with finding you in my bed, naked."

"I'll have to remember that," she murmured as she rubbed her cheek against his.

He held her close in an effort to ground his wayward emotions and soothe his Wolf. Her fingers stroked a spot on his chest as if she were petting a cat. The feel of her heartbeat and the warmth of her skin went a long way to calming him.

"One of those men called you Hotah. How come?" Her voice came out as little more than a whisper.

Of all the things she could have asked, he hadn't expected that. He was surprised she'd noticed with everything that had been going on.

"Hotah is my Sioux name."

"What does it mean?"

He smiled. *Always the scientist.* "Gray."

"Gray?"

He nodded.

"I realize it's stereotyping, but I thought a lot of Native American names came from animals or deeds or some kind of physical descriptor. Was your skin gray when you were born or something?"

He chuckled. "No. My grandfather had a vision not long after my mother told him she was pregnant with me. In his vision, he saw me walking with a gray wolf. He said this wolf would be significant to my life and would lead me in a new direction."

She stiffened in his arms. "A wolf?"

"Yes."

"Aren't wolves considered to be some premonition of evil?" Her voice quivered.

"Not at all. In many cultures, the wolf is considered a wise animal. One that is in touch with its intuition. It is thought to be a powerful spirit guide."

"Oh. I didn't realize that."

He had to ask. "You're a scientist. You study them

in the wild. Surely you aren't afraid of wolves."

She snorted. "God, no. But a lot of people are. And since I don't know much about the Sioux, I wasn't sure if that vision would be a good thing or a bad thing. Then again, I suppose it would be a good thing if you were named after something in the vision, right?" She spoke in such quick succession her words blurred together.

"Yes. That's right." He frowned. What had gotten into her?

She sat up. "I don't suppose you have something we can eat, do you? I'm starving."

"I'm sure we could find something." His brow furrowed as he rolled out of bed.

In the bathroom, he disposed of the condom then grabbed a pair of sweatpants and pulled them on. When he returned to the bedroom, he found Isabelle sitting in the middle of the bed, wearing his T-shirt and looking a little lost.

"Are you all right?"

"Yeah." She tugged at the edge of the shirt and grimaced. "It's been a bit of a crazy day."

"Yes it has." He went to the side of the bed and

pulled her to the edge. "But you survived and you're safe now, so don't let it get to you."

With the lightest of touches, he ran his finger over the red mark on her cheek. "I need to not look at that. Every time I do I want to rip Bob's spleen out." He balled his hand into a fist. "I'm already going to have a hard time explaining why he's missing two teeth and can't see out one eye."

She reached for his hand. "I didn't get a chance to thank you for saving me. Again."

In an instant, his anger fizzled. "You're welcome."

"Did they go to jail?"

"Oh, yes." He shrugged. "Well, after they make a pit stop at the hospital to get Bob patched up."

"Good. So it would be safe for me to return to my trailer tonight?"

He almost told her no but then remembered it was the first night of the full moon. It would be hard to explain why he stayed out all night. With reluctance, he told her, "Yes. You won't have to worry about Bob or Dalton bothering you again."

"Good. While I appreciate the use of your bathtub, I don't want to keep imposing on you. I'm sure I've created enough extra work for you."

He lifted her chin until she looked him in the eye. "You aren't extra work, Izzy. You are welcome to stay here if it makes you feel safer, but I won't be able to stay with you. I'm supposed to meet Drew and some friends, and it may take most of the night. I know that sounds terrible to ditch you after you've had such a traumatic day, but it's not something I can miss."

She smiled. "It's okay. Really." She pressed a kiss against the palm of his hand. "I kind of need to be in familiar surroundings, so I can collect my thoughts. I need to start packing, too. I'd only planned to be here five or six days. My dad will send the troops after me if I'm not home when he thinks I should be."

"Don't leave without telling me."

She grabbed the finger he pointed at her and kissed the tip. "I won't."

He looked deep into her eyes. Satisfied she wasn't just pacifying him, he relaxed. "Okay. Now, let's go see if we can whip up an omelet or something else worth eating."

"Yes, please."

Chapter Nine

Wyatt's meeting with Drew took longer than he wanted.

He liked the new Alpha, and he had pledged his loyalty, but it bothered him to have so much attention on Isabelle. The fact that two other single males had been ordered to keep an eye on her gnawed at him.

He didn't believe she would ever do anything to harm one of the pack, but since she didn't know the truth about them, there was the possibility she might report some obscure fact that could draw unwanted attention to Los Lobos.

Drew had reason to be concerned.

But dammit, he wasn't going to chase her off either. Besides, she already said she would be leaving soon. He needed to figure out how to get her to stay.

He locked his gun and holster in the special compartment of his truck. The moon pulled at him, and he wouldn't be able to fight the change much longer.

Besides, with his conflicted feelings, he needed a good run through the woods. Perhaps his Wolf would help him sort through the things that were bothering him.

In the distance, he heard a lone howl. It was answered by three or four.

Wyatt turned and greeted the moon as his grandfather had taught him. As he murmured his prayers to the spirits of his ancestors, he let the change wash over him then took off at a run for the woods.

Large paws pounded against the grass and dirt without hesitation.

Black fur rippled in the breeze.

Amber eyes scanned the area for prey and kin with heightened acuity.

Hotah caught up with his brothers on a ridge not far from Drew's property. They chased each other and a couple of rabbits and basked in the joy of simply being for a time. As the group circled around to the other end of Los Lobos, Hotah picked up an unexpected scent.

The rich smell of an unmated female filled his senses. He also detected something familiar. Something Hotah knew intimately but couldn't quite place.

Two of his pack mates detected it as well. The three of them stopped and inspected the area.

As soon as he locked onto the smell, Hotah took off to find the owner.

It was imperative he find her.

He ran as fast as he could while still following the trail. His brothers dropped away, hopefully losing interest. The trail led him to the river. There he found a lone silver-gray female drinking from the flowing water.

He circled around so he could approach from downwind. As he closed in, her undiluted scent hit him full blast.

Mate.

Lifting her head, she turned and met his gaze. Her

eyes glittered like the purest silver.

They studied each other warily as they circled ever closer until they nearly touched noses. At that close range, the familiarity grew stronger.

With fur bristled, he sniffed her from head to tail. The silver Wolf smelled of Isabelle.

But that wasn't possible.

Was it?

Shoulder to shoulder they stood, each assessing the other. Then the female gave in and nuzzled his cheek. Hotah, recognizing her acceptance, took a long, deep sniff of her muzzle. Her scent was ambrosia to his heightened Wolf senses.

Without warning, she took off running, encouraging him to give chase.

He wasn't about to let her out of his sight.

They wove in and out of the trees and bushes. Each time he got close, he nosed her haunches. Finally, she turned into his path, causing both of them to roll to the ground. Using his larger form, he pinned her then licked her face.

She returned his attentions with playful nips, growls, and nuzzling.

The appearance of three of his pack brothers interrupted their play.

Hotah sprang to his feet and bared his teeth, telling them he had staked his claim. They may be brothers, but he would fight any of them if they dared touch his mate.

The youngest of the three stepped forward and sniffed the air.

The silver Wolf rolled to her feet then stepped closer to Hotah, making it clear she had accepted him and was not open to another.

The foolish young Wolf took another step in her direction, forcing Hotah to counter him. Hotah exposed more teeth and let out a fiercer growl. Hotah was larger and far more experienced than the other. He didn't want to hurt his brother, but for her, he would take on the whole pack.

The other two Wolves backed away, leaving the younger Wolf to face Hotah's ire, if he dared. Giving in, he turned and followed his brethren.

The silver Wolf stepped forward and rubbed Hotah's neck with her nose.

Her attentions calmed him, but he watched the

trees to make sure the others had left. When he felt certain they were alone again, he licked her mouth and nose and rubbed against her.

They spent the rest of the night running and playing as wolves. Her acceptance of his Wolf smoothed a rough place in his soul he didn't realize he had.

Curled together, they fell asleep under a canopy of fallen pine limbs.

Hotah woke at dawn alone. He snarled and growled in protest then set off after her. Now that he had memorized her scent, he had no problem following her trail. It was no surprise it led to Isabelle's campsite.

Outside her trailer, he shifted from his Wolf form. He pounded on the door instead of kicking it in, as he would have liked.

"I don't know who you think you are coming in here, but you had best rethink it," she growled.

"It's me, Izzy."

"I'm trying to sleep. Come back later," she grumbled.

"I need sleep as well, and I plan on doing it with

you."

She opened the inner door and glared at him through the screen. "You simply decided that, huh?"

"I did." He opened the flimsy door and stepped inside, forcing her to step aside.

"What if I tell you I've never been able to sleep next to someone? That I'll toss and turn and keep you awake. Maybe even give you a few bruises in the process."

She had wrapped a sheet around her, but it did little to conceal her nakedness beneath. There were at least two of his single pack mates patrolling nearby. "You could tell me you breathe fire in your sleep and I still wouldn't leave."

She frowned. "It doesn't mean it's a good idea for you to be here."

"Yeah, well, word of a breedable female shifter being in the area will have spread like wildfire, and I'm not about to leave you alone."

She lifted her chin a notch.

"Two of our bachelors are already hot on your trail. More will probably show up before noon. I don't think you realize how tenuous of a position you're in here."

She stomped toward the bed. "I can take care of myself."

He followed. "Not against a pack you can't."

She whipped her heard around. Her eyes were wide with concern. "There's a whole pack here? How big?"

He snapped his jaw shut.

"Oh, come on. There's no point in having secrets now. I know what you are. You know what I am...."

"We have a lot to discuss, but until I've talked with my Alpha, I am bound by oath to not betray the pack." He reached for the buttons on his shirt. "Right now, we both need sleep."

"You're really going to stay here? With me?"

"I thought I made that clear when I came in."

"Will you answer my questions when we get up?"

"After I've talked to the Alpha."

She chewed her lower lip. "Fine. Sleep first. Talk later."

He finished working the buttons loose on his shirt as Isabelle climbed onto the extended platform. The sheet fell to her lap, exposing her breasts as she rearranged the pillows. And just like that, he was hard again. What was it about this woman that turned him into a sex-starved idiot?

He sat on the edge of the bed and removed his boots. Next, he made a pile of his jeans, briefs, and shirt. He crawled under the sheet and got comfortable on his side. He wrapped an arm around Izzy's waist, pulled her against his chest then caged her in with his leg.

She squirmed enough to make him reconsider his thought of sleeping first. She must have realized what she was doing by wigging her bottom against his growing erection and went still. They would have time later to work on that problem.

With a sigh of contentment, he closed his eyes and fell asleep to the feel of his mate's heartbeat beneath his palm.

Chapter Ten

I sabelle woke feeling as if the furnace had been turned on high and aimed at her back. She squirmed and tried to roll over, but something held her in place.

Her brain broke through the fog of sleep, and she remembered where she was. And more importantly, who slept with her.

Wyatt.

And he was a shifter.

Like her.

Damn if that didn't beat all.

But now what?

She smiled to herself and wiggled her butt against his crotch. In a matter of seconds, that part of his body responded.

Despite the weight of his arm around her chest, she managed to turn so she faced his chest. With an unhurried stroke of her tongue, she tasted him. *Salty.* The musk of his Wolf clung to his skin and called to her other form.

Without fear of an unexpected shift, she inhaled, drawing his scent in as far as she could. With her hampered sense of smell, it took a lot for anything to register.

Trailing her fingers over his skin, she traced patterns over his chest then down his side to his hip. There she switched directions and lightly scraped her nails over the curve of his ass. It was a very fine ass. She loved the way it looked in jeans, but it was positively delectable naked. If she were in a better position, she'd take a few nibbles.

Enjoying the freedom to explore his body as she wanted, she ran her fingers through the hair on his thigh, then up to his groin. She teased the edges of his now considerable erection then ran her palm down the entire length.

A rumble in his chest was her only warning before he rolled her onto her back and settled between her thighs.

"It's not wise to tease wild animals. You can never be sure of what they may do."

"I hope I know exactly what you're going to do."

He swiveled his hips and maneuvered his cock to her opening. He held her gaze, then sank into her as if he had all the time in the world.

Isabelle's lips parted, and she took a deep breath.

The intimacy of being connected visually and physically warmed her soul. In her heart, something clicked into place.

At least they didn't have to worry about condoms anymore. Since they were both Wolves, they couldn't contract human diseases, and she wouldn't get pregnant until she decided to.

She hummed with pleasure. Skin-to-skin contact far outweighed having that thin membrane between them.

Wyatt took his time. Every slide of his cock made her want him more. With deliberate slowness, he caressed her. Loved her. She could swear there was devotion in all of his touches.

Her heart prayed she wasn't imaging things.

With their bodies still joined, he pulled her legs up until her feet were above his shoulders, next to his face. "Now, keep your eyes open. I want you to see who is buried inside of you. Deeper than anyone has ever been."

Isabelle felt the first stirrings of her orgasm but wanted him to come with her. "Wyatt," she whimpered.

"Yes," he hissed, then adjusted the angle of his thrust. But it was enough to hit the right spot and send her flying.

She grasped his arms and tried to keep eye contact, but she could see nothing but stars behind her eyes. With a keening, cry she surrendered to the feeling. She rode wave after wave of pleasure and barely noticed when he groaned and shuddered with his own release.

Wyatt slumped onto the mattress next to her then rolled and pulled her on top of him.

Isabell lay sprawled across his chest and listened to the hammering of his heart as it struggled to return to normal. Her own beat in a similar fashion.

As the euphoria wore off, questions flooded her

brain. He couldn't be the only shifter here, so how many of them lived nearby? Where had they come from? And how long had they been here?

"Were you going to tell me?" Wyatt interrupted her growing list of questions.

Her brows drew together in a frown. "What? That I had a strange family trait?" She lifted her head and looked him in the eye. "What about you? Were you planning to tell me?"

He grunted. "If we were mated, of course I would have."

"Well, then, you have your answer." She lay her head down on his chest.

"How did you learn about us?"

"I didn't. I suspected a pack might be in the area, but I didn't know where."

"So, you didn't come here looking for Los Lobos?"

"For what?"

"Los Lobos. The town where most of our pack lives."

She shook her head. "No. I told you. I tracked some wolves from the park in Georgia." She sighed and then sat up. "What I didn't tell you was I was looking for one specific wolf."

Wyatt's body tensed at her words.

"A young wolf, a female, got caught in a poacher's trap in the park I worked in. My assistant and I found her. Her leg and paw were damaged not only from the trap, but from her efforts to get out. To make it worse, it looked as if she had been attacked by another wolf or something large either before ending up in the trap or while captive." She looked away. "I tranquilized her and took her to my lab so we could treat her. While she was under, I put a tracking chip in her shoulder. I collected data on her whereabouts for about two weeks. After that, nothing."

"And that data led you here."

She nodded.

"Why were you tracking her?"

"It's what I do. I study wolves and their habitat and the correlation between them. One of the ways we do that is to follow their movements. Later, after running a few blood tests, I realized the wolf I'd saved wasn't an ordinary wolf."

He tensed again. "What did you find?"

"It's a marker of some kind at a DNA level that I

think all shifters have."

He sat up and leaned on his elbow, his eyes narrowed.

She continued. "I have it, my brother has it, and so do my mom and dad and many of my pack mates."

"Your parents are both shifters?"

She nodded.

"Your brother, too?"

"Of course. Why do you seem surprised by that?"

He clamped his lips shut then shuffled out from underneath the sheet.

"What's wrong?" she asked.

"We need to find Drew."

"Drew? Why?"

"I can only tell you that I cannot answer any of your questions until I've talked with Drew."

"He's your Alpha, isn't he?"

A voice called from outside her trailer. "Yes, he is, and he would like to speak with you. Both of you."

Wyatt grabbed his jeans, pulling them on while Isabelle wrapped the sheet around herself. He strode to the door and stuck his head out.

"Hotah. I understand you had a rather"—the man

paused—"engaging evening last night."

"Drew." He stepped out but blocked the doorway with his broad frame. "I expected you sooner."

"There were a few things to take care of on the home front first. I assume you'll introduce me to your friend?"

Wyatt blocked Isabelle's view out of the narrow closure. "She isn't dressed for visitors."

"I suggest that she do it quickly," Drew said. "We have things to discuss."

"Yes, we do, but I had hoped to arrange a meeting time," he suggested.

Drew's voice dropped. "There are a handful of unmated pack mates tracking her scent as we speak. I also have a few angry Sentries who want to know how she got so close to pack land without them knowing about it. Right now, the only thing keeping all of them from barging in here is the fact you were seen with her last night and this morning."

Wyatt growled.

Isabelle pushed Wyatt out of the way so she could see Drew's face. Wyatt tried to block her once again, but she smacked his arm and pushed him to the side.

"I'm afraid I don't understand. Why do your pack mates care that I'm here, and what do they have to be angry about?"

Drew's brow arched, and he looked from Wyatt to Isabelle and back again. "How much does she know about us?"

"Nothing," Isabelle answered at the same time as Wyatt.

"You'll recall I'm under oath to not disclose anything about the pack to outsiders," he reminded Drew.

"And you stuck to that oath?" He clapped Wyatt on the shoulder. "Good job. No one else does."

"I don't take oaths lightly," Wyatt said without a smile or any hint of amusement.

"Not everyone feels the same way you do," Drew pointed out. To Isabelle he ordered, "Get dressed."

Her brows rose. "Excuse me?" She looked at Wyatt. "Is he ordering me around?"

A rumble sounded in Drew's chest. Wyatt stepped between them.

"She is not rogue. She has an Alpha." He looked to Isabelle for confirmation. "Your father, I'm guessing?"

"Yes," she answered curter than she intended.

A tall, curvy redheaded woman stepped out of the trees and into the clearing. She called out, "Ignore his bad manners. He had to get up a little earlier than he wanted this morning, and that always makes him cranky."

Drew's face softened when he looked at the woman. The redhead must be someone special to him. "I am not cranky," he protested.

"Yes, you are and don't bother denying it." The woman smiled at Isabelle. "Hi. I'm Betty, Drew's mate." She offered her hand in greeting. "It's nice to meet you."

Isabelle pulled the sheet tighter then shook hands with Betty. "It's nice to meet you, too. I'm Isabelle."

"Isabelle. What a pretty name." She elbowed Drew in the side. "Isn't that a pretty name?"

Drew grunted. "Yeah, uh-huh."

Betty's gaze flitted around the campsite then settled on Isabelle and Wyatt. "You interrupted them, didn't you, Drew?"

Isabelle answered for him. "Yes. He did."

She shook her head then linked an arm through Drew's. "Come on. Let's go make everyone some coffee and give them a chance to get dressed."

Drew gestured to the trees around them. "Did you not see half the pack circling the area? We have a potential riot on our hands. We need to figure out what to do about it."

"And we will. But it can wait until they've had a chance to get dressed and maybe eat a bite. Actually, I have a better idea." To Isabelle and Wyatt she suggested, "Why don't the two of you come out to the house and have lunch with us?"

"Er...." Isabelle looked to Wyatt for his reaction.

He tipped his head to Betty. "That's most generous of you."

They agreed on a time, and then Betty tugged on Drew's arm. "Let's go see what those guard dogs of yours are carrying on about."

"Guard dogs?" Drew asked in disbelief. He sighed then followed Betty.

"He's a different person when he's around Betty," Wyatt mumbled as he watched the departing couple.

"People say the same thing about my dad,"

Isabelle said as she entered the trailer.

He grunted then went in search of his shirt.

"I need a bath. Do you want to join me?" She raised her brow in question and let the sheet fall to the ground.

He raked his gaze over her naked form.

That rumbling sound he made when he became aroused sent goose bumps down both arms and made warmth pool between her legs. It took no time for him to shed his jeans and tumble her onto the bed.

It took a full half hour to gather their clothes and head to Wyatt's place for a shower.

Chapter Eleven

Isabelle and Wyatt arrived at Drew's place with only minutes to spare. They'd been together twice today, yet he wanted nothing more than to pull the truck over and drag her across the console.

He'd been told sex was different between mates. It was hotter and eased the loneliness they all carried deep within. If there were any doubts of Isabelle being his mate, that fact alone erased them.

"Are you okay? You're awfully quiet." Isabelle frowned with concern.

"Sorry. I'm fine. Just a lot on my mind."

"Are you worried about meeting with Drew? Is there something I should know ahead of time?"

"No." He patted her leg. "I'm sure lunch will be

fine. Betty will ensure that."

They pulled into the drive and parked. On the way up to the house, she slipped her hand into his. A warm feeling spread through his chest and made him smile.

Drew greeted them at the door. "Ah. Good." He gestured for them to enter. "I'm starved."

Betty was drying her hands on a towel when she entered the room. "Great timing. I just finished the potato salad. Come on in." She tugged Isabelle toward the hallway. "I hope you like hamburgers. If not, we have turkey patties we can grill."

"Hamburgers are fine with me."

Their voices trailed off as they went farther down the hall.

Drew pulled Wyatt to a stop. "All right, before we go in, tell me the truth. What's going on between the two of you?"

"With all due respect, that's none of your business."

"That is where you're wrong. You spent the better part of a week in her company but didn't say anything about her being a shifter. Either you didn't know or weren't saying for some reason. So, before there is any discussion of the pack, I need to know if you're willing to claim her and take full responsibility for her."

That was what he'd been asking himself all day.

"You realize you're asking me a question that I haven't discussed with her yet, don't you?"

"Not my problem. The pack is. And I need to know. Because if you don't want her, I'm sure one of the others—"

"Yes," Wyatt growled and puffed his chest. "Yes. I am willing. If anyone else so much as looks at her the wrong way, they will have to face me."

Drew smiled. "Okay. Just checking." He clasped Wyatt on the shoulder. "Now, let's eat."

Instead of the dining room, Drew led him to the kitchen where he found an informal spread of hamburgers and toppings for them, some fruit, and a couple of sides.

"There you two are. I was beginning to think you'd taken off," Betty said.

"Are you kidding? I'm starving after slaving over the grill for the last hour," Drew grumbled.

"So you've been reminding me for the last fifteen minutes," Betty said under her breath. "Grab a plate and dig in."

Isabelle and Wyatt exchanged glances. He gave her a nod to reassure her everything was fine. He handed a plate to her then proceeded to fill his own, stopping occasionally to help Isabelle.

Once they sat down, it didn't take Drew long to turn the conversation to the topic he wanted to discuss.

"So, Isabelle, tell us where you're from."

She repeated the same information she had already given Wyatt about her home in Georgia and her family.

"And your pack?" Drew prompted.

"Last count we were almost five hundred strong."

Drew's brow rose in surprise.

"Wow," Betty exclaimed. "I didn't realize there were so many in the state much less in one area. What'd your dad do, take over the four closest packs?"

"Not exactly. But he did incorporate the business about ten years ago after he bought out his biggest competitor, and it's been growing ever since. All of his seconds work there along with a great many members of the pack in some capacity or another. Pack members are always the preferred hire, so we draw them from the entire area. Between the contracts they've landed in the last two years, the spin-off companies he's created, and the income the corporation has reinvested, Dad figures we could be self-sustaining for several years even if Wall Street crashed and burned."

Drew's fork stalled halfway to his mouth. "Truly self-sustaining?"

"Seriously?" Betty asked at the same time.

"Uh-huh," Isabelle said then took another bite. "Betty this is great potato salad. You need to send me your recipe."

"Okay, so what I want to know is why didn't we smell your Wolf on you?" Wyatt pushed his plate aside. "I didn't detect it at all," he grumbled.

"Good question," Drew said.

"Oh, that's Mom's doing," Isabelle said as if that explained everything. Instead, she had three sets of blank looks. "Mom is a biophysicist. She's been working on something to tone down the natural pheromones we produce. Originally, she made it to mitigate the aggressive subconscious response humans have to our race. Her theory is that humans, whenever they are around our kind, whether or not they realize it, have hostile tendencies toward us. She speculates it's because they fear us on a primal level."

"Go on," Drew encouraged.

"She thought if she could find a way to mask our natural predatory scent, we would have better chances in the business world. They may still be seen as a corporation to be feared but not because of any wild pheromones we're emitting."

"Well, didn't you pick up on Wyatt's natural scent?"

"No, I didn't." She grimaced. "That was the side effect of Mom's first formula. Not only is my scent neutralized, but my sense of smell is greatly diminished."

"That kinda sucks," Betty murmured.

"I figure it's a small price to pay in return for being able to be out in the wilds and not have all the animals I study smell me coming and run away."

"Oh, my God, I didn't think of that. That would make it hard to be a wildlife biologist, wouldn't it?" Betty guessed.

"Yes, it did." Isabelle sat back in her chair. "My first year doing field work was frustrating. It was rare that I was able to find families to study. My professors didn't believe I was doing my research when I repeatedly returned with no results. My second year was spent working in groups and even then it was with little results." She took a sip of her tea. "I spent the summer crying on my mother's shoulders about my grades and how I was going to get thrown out of the program all because of a stupid gene that I didn't ask for. So my mom took it upon herself to speed up research she was already working on and developed a product to help me."

Drew and Wyatt exchanged looks.

"And obviously it works," Betty pointed out.

"Yes, it does. It's not perfect, there are a couple of side effects she's still working through, but all in all, those of us who have tried it have been happy with it."

"You were one of your mother's test subjects?"

Wyatt's voice rumbled when he spoke.

"Of course. Who else better to test it?"

"Oh, I don't know, perhaps lab rats? Or maybe prisoners who have been convicted of raping and killing children? But not you. Her own daughter." The more Wyatt thought of Isabelle being forced to submit to a product test galled him.

Betty and Drew watched their interaction.

"Why not? Do you think I should have waited until it was being sold over the counter at the local Walmart?"

"Yes."

Isabelle crossed her arms over her chest. "God, you sound like Dad."

Wyatt blinked in surprise.

"And Lewis."

Wyatt growled, "Who is Lewis?"

She narrowed her eyes in warning. "You can tuck that macho-male attitude away. What difference does it make who Lewis is?"

"Answer me."

"Do we need to leave the two of you alone?" Betty grinned.

"No." Isabelle and Wyatt both answered at the same time.

"Okay good. So, when was your last heat?" Betty pressed.

"B, that's not polite dinner conversation," Drew pointed out.

"Why not?" she protested. "This morning, I had to threaten to drag two of the younger males home by their ears. All because they thought there was an unmated female within pissing distance. They're not usually that annoying."

Wyatt growled again. Their questioning was getting way too personal. He wasn't sure how much more he could take.

Isabelle's eyes widened. "You mean me?"

"I'm afraid so," Betty confirmed.

Drew shook his head in dismay.

"Don't worry." Betty waved a hand in Isabelle's direction. "Once word spreads that you're with Wyatt, they'll leave you alone."

"But I...." Isabelle looked at Wyatt, her eyes wide with concern. "But we haven't...." She bit her lip.

Wyatt stifled his impulse to pull Isabelle into his

lap. "We have a lot of things to discuss."

"Oh." Betty looked to Drew then at Isabelle and Wyatt. "Sorry. I just assumed...."

Wyatt held Isabelle's gaze. "Who is Lewis?"

Isabelle rolled her eyes. "My brother."

Pacified by her answer, he relaxed once again. "So this formula of your mother's, does it work on all shifters?"

"She hasn't tested it on other breeds of shifters yet, like bear or panther shifters, but she thinks it would work the same. It's been a matter of not having a volunteer from either of those packs step up."

Wyatt nudged her arm. "Do you think it would work on me?"

Isabelle frowned. "Most likely, but why would you need it?"

Drew and Betty wore similar expressions of confusion.

He smiled. "Did you not wonder why we rode four-wheelers at George's place instead of horses? Like most tourists?"

"No. Well, after seeing all of the beautiful horses I did. But that thought only lasted about a second."

"All the years I worked for George I was never able to ride a horse without either wearing myself and the horse out in a struggle for control or I would get bucked off. I always suspected my Wolf half made the horses nervous."

"You sure it's not because you're a lousy cowboy?" Drew smarted off.

Wyatt shook his head, refusing to rise to the bait. "Even the most docile of horses wanted nothing to do with me."

"I don't see why it wouldn't work on you. We can ask Mother." She tipped her head. "She'd want to check you over first, though. Which would require you to go to Georgia."

"I've never been to Georgia. I think I'd like to see it."

Something passed between them. Something unspoken. A promise of sorts, perhaps.

But there would be time later to figure it out.

Chapter Twelve

Betty cleared her throat. "Speaking of Georgia. What brought you all the way out here?"

"I tracked a wolf I encountered earlier this year to this area," Isabelle said.

"Wyatt told us what you said when you arrived. But I want to know the real reason you came," Drew said bluntly.

"Er...." Isabelle looked to Wyatt with a question in her eye. He nodded for her to continue.

She played with the water droplets on the outside of her glass as she told them about the young wolf she had helped.

"You said you found this wolf caught in a trap?" Drew cocked his head to the side. "Was it a coyote trap?"

"It was one of those horrible things with two jaws that snaps shut around the animal's paws." Isabelle motioned with her hands how the thing closed.

Betty cringed. "Did the wolf you freed have a diamond-shaped mark around her right eye?"

Isabelle sat up straighter in her seat. "Yes, she did."

"And did she injure her"-Drew paused and looked to Betty for confirmation but she only gave him a blank stare in return-"left front paw?"

Isabelle dug through memories. "Yes, I believe she did. Do you know her?"

Drew's eyes narrowed with suspicion. "Why are you so interested in that particular wolf?"

"I'd like to find out if she's okay and if she suffered permanent injury from the trap. I did the best I could for her, but I'm no doctor. I also wanted to confirm my suspicions."

Drew's brow rose in question.

"That she is a shifter and belongs to a pack I am unfamiliar with."

"What made you think she was a shifter?" Betty

asked.

"First of all, I left her sedated in a cage in my lab for the night. When we found her missing the next morning, I pulled surveillance tapes to make sure no one had taken her or done something to her. The tape showed a young girl with a pronounced limp leaving the building."

Based on the looks Betty and Drew exchanged, she would bet money they knew the girl.

"There's more," Wyatt added.

"While she was sedated, I implanted a tracking chip in her shoulder," Isabelle confessed.

"You what?" Drew roared and sat up in his chair.

Wyatt leaned forward and tried to place himself between her and Drew. She patted him on the shoulder to reassure him that Drew's outburst didn't bother her. She was used to loud, dominant men. She had grown up around two of them and, thanks to her father's friends and business partners, she'd learned how to deal with them early in life.

But it was sweet of him to be concerned for her. "It is common practice in my field to use tracking chips because it's a fast and easy ways to collect data on animal movement," she explained.

"You did it even though you suspected she was a shifter?"

"God, no." She gave Drew a disgruntled look. "If you'll recall what I said, it wasn't until the next day that I had any reason to suspect she was anything other than Canis lupus."

Wyatt smiled.

Drew grunted in response.

"Once Mother confirmed the likelihood of the wolf being a shifter, I kept tabs on her movements through the chip. I tracked her as far as the Black Hills, but then the signal died."

Betty frowned. "Wait. How did your mother learn she was a shifter?"

"From the blood I took from the wolf." She held her hand up to stop any yelling Drew might do. "Again, before I suspected anything." She looked at Betty. "Years ago, Mother found an anomaly that showed up on certain DNA strands that all wolf shifters have in common. It's quite small and, unless you know what you're looking for, you probably wouldn't notice it. After seeing the video footage, I sent the blood I had taken over to Mother." She shrugged. "If there was a chance of her being a shifter, I didn't want it getting mixed up with any of the other lab specimens."

"Is this anomaly something anyone with access to our blood and microscope could see?" Betty asked, alarmed.

"No. It's too small to be seen with a regular microscope. It takes special equipment to be found and, like I said, you'd have to know what you're looking for. Besides, this isn't something Mother has published a paper about. That is a well-guarded secret. Very few people have seen her research. I have only seen the marker a time or two, and that was after Mother isolated and magnified it. I doubt I'd be able to find it on my own."

"But this wolf you found had it?" Drew clarified.

"Yes, she did."

Drew leaned forward in his chair. "What does someone's DNA tell you about them?"

"Well, DNA can tell you who is related to whom, like parent to child. It tells whether or not the subject is male or female, a great many physical characteristics like hair and eye color and whether the subject is likely to develop certain diseases."

Betty's eyes widened in surprise. "All of that?"

Isabelle nodded.

"What about insanity?" Drew's voice was just above a whisper. "Can it tell you whether or not you're prone to insanity?"

Isabelle looked to Wyatt. He nodded for her to continue. "Er, not that I'm aware of."

Betty put her hand on Drew's and squeezed.

"So, now what?" Wyatt prompted.

"Now, I want to hear what she plans to do with the information she has collected about our pack," Drew said.

"I hope you realize that I have not been studying your pack and have little information on it as a whole. Being a shifter myself, and daughter to our pack leader, I understand the need for privacy and security for the safety of all. I can assure you I have no plans to do any formal research on you or your pack members."

Drew started to say something, but once again, she held her hand up to stop him. Wyatt grinned from behind his cup.

"As a scientist, I cannot help but observe and collect data. But that doesn't mean I will use the information for anything more than my own curiosity. Now"—she paused—"that said, if I found the information could be used to benefit both of our packs, I reserve the right to bring it up to both parties."

Drew narrowed his gaze. "What do you mean?"

"I mean if I observe some environmental factor that could impact either of our packs negatively, then I would think you would want to be informed of it. Am I correct?"

"Absolutely," Drew said.

"Okay, then."

"So, you're not going to write a research paper on us then," Betty confirmed.

"Certainly not. But, with your permission, I would like to be able to speak to my mother and father about you and your pack."

Drew's gaze narrowed. "Why?"

"For starters, to make them aware of another pack's existence. Father has contacts in most of the packs along the East Coast. I think he would be excited to meet you. Allies are a good thing. And you never know when a partnership in a new venture could be formed."

"Let me think about that," Drew mumbled.

"As for Mother, she's always looking for bright new talent for her research team. If any of your young people show an aptitude in the sciences, she has established scholarships in exchange for their agreement to work on one of her teams or in the main laboratory."

"I assume you mean as a researcher, not as a lab specimen," Betty said with the lift of one brow.

"Of course. Mother has a division devoted to the development of medicines and products for our kind, and it's a requirement everyone be either a shifter or a descendant of a shifter."

"Did you inherit your Wolf from your father's line?" Drew inquired.

"Both my mother and my father."

"I did some research on you and your family when you showed up," Drew said without remorse. "If you think he'd be open to it, I would like to meet your father. He's made some impressive changes with his spin-off companies. I wouldn't mind talking with him about how he's managed to grow his business while maintaining pack security and secrecy."

"I'll let him know."

"What about you? Surely, you have questions," Wyatt suggested.

"Actually, I do, if you don't mind me prying," Isabelle admitted.

Drew gestured for her to proceed.

"Based on your reactions, I'm guessing the wolf I found belongs to your pack. What was a young girl doing so far from home? And alone, no less."

Drew looked at Wyatt then to Betty. He took a deep breath, then said, "In a nutshell, my father."

Isabelle's brow drew up in question.

"It's a long sordid story what my father put this pack through. Suffice to say abuse was rampant and several pack members ran away." Drew tapped his finger on the table. "I believe the wolf you found was indeed one of ours. Her name is Lucy. A scout found her and her mother in Iowa and encouraged them to return home after reassuring them that Magnum was no longer in charge."

Betty picked up the story. "Lucy left with her mother a few months before Magnum was killed. There's no telling what the poor woman went through. Her husband had been killed, and back then, women without a mate were, well, vulnerable.

"Lucy said they had been staying with her mom's aunt and uncle when the change hit her for the first time. Poor thing. Her mom was so tangled in her own issues she couldn't help Lucy." Betty looked at Wyatt then Isabelle. "We believe it was only a couple of moons later when she became caught in the trap you mentioned."

"Oh poor thing," Isabelle murmured.

"Not that it was a good thing, but it scared her mother enough to return. By then, Magnum was gone."

"Is Lucy all right now?" Isabelle hoped so.

Betty nodded. "Yes. We sent her to a doctor soon after she and her mother returned and we learned of her injury. We were assured that because she was young and still growing, there would be no lingering damage."

The tension she didn't realize she had been carrying eased. "Good."

Drew spoke up. "The doctor also told us that had she not been let out of that trap and the bleeding stopped, there would have been lasting damage. And if she had shifted while still in the trap it's likely the major artery that runs down the leg might have been damaged and she could have bled to death."

Betty added, "Basically, you saved Lucy's life."

Isabelle's heart leaped.

"And for that we are grateful," Drew said. "Our pack isn't as large as yours and our young ones should be treasured. That is something I am hoping to stress to everyone in Los Lobos."

"Would it be possible for me to see her?" Isabelle asked hopefully.

Betty and Drew exchanged looks.

"I don't see why you can't," Betty finally answered. "I'll talk to her mother and see if we can arrange it."

Isabelle smiled. "That would be great."

Now that they had resolved the sensitive topics, they were able to relax and enjoy dessert. By the time they left, Isabelle felt as if she wouldn't have to tiptoe around Wyatt. And perhaps he would be candid with her in return.

Chapter Thirteen

After lunch, Wyatt and Isabelle returned to her trailer. Wyatt walked the perimeter of her campsite to make sure they had plenty of privacy. Satisfied they were alone, he took a seat under her canopy.

She handed him a bottle of water. "So, what did Drew mean when he asked if you would take responsibility for me?"

"You heard that?"

She nodded. "My sense of smell may not be what it should, but my hearing is great."

After taking a deep breath, he explained. "In Los Lobos, if a pack member brings a human in and accepts them as their mate, the human must promise to keep pack secrets. The pack member is required to accept responsibility for them."

She took a seat next to him. "But I'm not human. Does the same rule apply to me?"

"To a certain degree." He tapped the side of his bottle. "You're a shifter, so you understand the need for secrecy where humans are concerned. But you aren't a member of the Los Lobos Pack, so there are still some things that should remain secret." He sighed. "And while you're here you would be expected to follow pack rules."

She tipped her head to the side. "Does that mean you have to watch me at all times?"

Wyatt frowned, unsure of where her question might be leading. "It means if you break any pack laws, then punishment will be delivered to me."

"So, you made a commitment to your Alpha?"

"Yes."

"About me."

"Yes."

"Without talking to me about it first?"

"Er...." It occurred to him he was on shaky ground.

"What exactly does this commitment involve?" she pressed.

"It can be whatever we want it to be," he suggested.

"You don't have to ask your Alpha?"

"No. This is between you and me."

She got up and walked to the edge of the canopy and looked into the thickness of the surrounding trees. He couldn't see her face and worried what she might be thinking.

"So, I could return to Atlanta as long as I promise not to tell anyone other than Mom and Dad about the pack."

His gut clenched. "Yes," he said through gritted teeth.

She looked at him. "What about you?"

"What about me?"

She closed the distance between them. "Do you plan to always be at your Alpha's beck and call?"

He smiled. She wasn't holding back, was she? "I'm not at my Alpha's beck and call now. I am my own man. I don't live in Los Lobos. I am not dependent on the pack for survival. I choose to support the new Alpha because he is a good man and I believe he can bring the pack to life again and repair the damage his father did." He put the bottle on the table behind him. "I keep Drew informed of events that may impact the pack, and I warn him of possible dangers. But my day-to-day life is my own." He took her hands in his. "Yes, I have family and friends in the pack but the reality is, I could move to Alaska and the pack would survive. So would I."

"How do you feel about starting your own family?" she asked, then bit her lip.

Wyatt's brain stalled.

His own family.

A beautiful wife. A mate for life. Young ones to raise and play with in the yard. His heart warmed at the thought. "I'd never allowed myself to think much about it." He added, "Until recently."

"But you may want that? Some day?"

"Yes. I would."

"And, uh, what would you want in a mate?"

He pulled her into his lap and pushed a strand of her hair behind her ear. "She'd have to be smart, spirited, witty enough to keep me on my toes. And she'd have to enjoy the outdoors."

She tipped her head to the side. "What? No

physical requirements like big boobs or flaxen hair?"

"A beautiful heart is all that matters. That being said...." He ran his hand down the front of her shirt then slipped it beneath the hem so he could feel the softness of her skin. "It wouldn't hurt if she were flexible enough to get into some of the Kama Sutra positions I've always wanted to try."

Isabelle gave him a sultry smile. "Like the lotus blossom, perhaps?"

"Is that the one where you have your legs crossed in front of you?"

She nibbled the side of is his mouth. "Uh-huh."

"Yeah. That would be good to try."

Isabelle whispered. "I do a lot of yoga. Advanced yoga. So I'm pretty flexible."

"I'm very glad to hear that."

She put her hand on his chest and leaned away. "Let me ask you this. If you found the right woman, would you chase her all the way to Georgia to be with her?"

"I'd follow *you* through the gates of hell."

Her smile lit up her face. "Good because Georgia does get pretty hot in the summer."

He put every ounce of feeling he had into the kiss he gave her. She was his mate. He had to make her see how much he wanted her. How much he needed her in his life. Now that he'd found her, he wasn't about to let her go.

She shivered in his arms. "Wyatt," she murmured against his lips. "Take me inside."

He lifted her into his arms and carried her to the door. Since neither of them wanted to let go and neither was willing to take their lips off the other, he fumbled with the latch and they stumbled inside. By the time they found the bed, they were laughing between kisses.

They fell onto the mattress, pulling at each other's clothes. Their urgency made it harder to get the barriers out of the way so they could be skin to skin. He finally grabbed her wrists and pinned them above her head. That only inflamed her.

She wound her legs around his hips as she nipped at his chin.

"Dammit, Izzy," he growled. His control was close to snapping and neither of them was naked. "You get me so worked up."

"It's only fair," she murmured against his neck as she licked and kissed what she could reach.

He captured her lips and pressed her into the mattress. When he released her he said, "Okay, I'm going to let go so you can get your clothes off and I'll get mine. Deal?" He kissed her again.

She grinned. "Deal."

God, she was sexy with her hair awry and her cheeks flushed with passion.

"All right. Go." He rolled off her and pulled his shirt over his head. He sent it sailing toward the end of the bed, then went to work on his jeans. In record time, he had everything pushed off, including his socks.

He turned to grab Isabelle, but she flung herself into his arms. Flesh met flesh and lips found lips. He rolled her beneath him and did his damnedest to gain some foothold in their coupling but Izzy was having none of that. She squirmed and caressed and fondled making him wild with need.

"Now, Wyatt. I need you inside of me."

"Not until you come."

He scooted down the mattress, leaving tiny bite

marks as he went. When he reached the area he wanted, he pulled her knees up so her bent legs pressed against her belly. There, he had the perfect view of her pussy. The bright pink flesh dripped with her desire. Knowing she was ready and anxious for him heightened his need.

With no preamble, he buried his face in her heat and licked in earnest. At the first touch of his tongue, she gasped and grabbed at the sheets. He showed her no mercy. There was no teasing and no feathery touches. He wanted to hear her greedy whimpers and to feel her pulling at his hair begging for more.

Back and forth he worked his tongue over her clit. When he closed his lips around it and suckled, she grabbed his head and clamped down with her thighs. Finally, she went stiff and the muscles in her legs began to quiver.

"Oh God, Wyatt," she cried.

The taste of her filled his mouth. He lapped it up as if it were the sweetest ambrosia.

She was still ridding the tidal wave of pleasure when he positioned his cock at her opening and sank into her. Her tight channel quivered around him, pushing him closer to the brink.

"Open your eyes, Izzy," he demanded.

They were only slits, but he knew she had complied. "You are my mate. Accept me. Accept my Wolf. We accept you."

He dropped the last of his mental barriers and opened his soul to her, praying she could and would accept his offering.

She gasped. "Wyatt."

Awe replaced confusion as their mating bond snapped into place.

The warmth of her love filled that empty place in his heart. In return, he pushed everything he felt but had never been able to find words for to her through their newly formed connection. Her eyes widened then teared up with joy.

Mate.

The word echoed in both of their minds.

Love me, she whispered.

Always, he declared, then proceeded to show her with his body how much.

Epilogue

"I'm surprised your mother recovered from her cold so fast," Isabelle told Wyatt as they slipped out onto his patio, away from the crowd.

"Me, too. She took all the herbs Grandfather brought her and didn't complain more than once. So I guess she really wanted to be here."

"Dinner wouldn't have been the same without her." She grinned. "And wasn't Lucy beautiful tonight? Her poor mother is going to have to beat the boys away with a stick before long."

"That's true."

"It's been wonderful getting to know Lucy. She is such a sweet young woman." She steered Wyatt into a dark corner of the porch and wrapped her arms around his neck. "Thank you for hosting the dinner tonight. I think it will be good if our two packs can form an alliance."

"You're welcome. I'm glad your job allows you to work remotely and that you were able to stay."

"You don't mind that my dad showed up without warning?"

"It was a little uncomfortable that first morning. But I can't say as I blame him." He pulled Isabelle closer and nuzzled her neck. "If I were lucky enough to be blessed with a beautiful daughter, I'd do the same thing if she suddenly announced she'd found her mate."

Her knees went weak, as they always did when he kissed her on that sensitive spot below her ear.

"Thank you for—" She gasped when he flicked a thumb across her breast. "For being so patient with him while he grilled you."

He raised his head. "Don't think I've forgotten what you said, though."

She had trouble remembering her own name whenever he kissed her much less anything else. "What's that?"

"That you owed me an evening of sensual delights to make up for your dad's visit."

"Oh, I haven't forgotten. After Dad and his entourage leave, I plan to give you something to remember for a long while." She pulled him down and sealed her promise with a kiss.

About the Author

Dena Garson is a Process Redesign Specialist by day and a writer and jewelry designer by night. She is raising two rowdy boys who play lots of sports which forces her to spend way to much time on the practice field and/or sidelines. Thankfully she has a loyal and loving Labrador Retriever to listen when she complains.